SHADOWED TREASURES

Jennifer J. Morgan

Books by Jennifer J. Morgan

Libby Madsen Cozy Mysteries

Shadows in the Forest
Spa Shadows
Shadowed Treasures
Shadow Retreats (fall/winter 2022)
The Christmas Fairy - a holiday novella

SHADOWED TREASURES

Libby Madsen Cozy Mysteries, Book 3

Jennifer J. Morgan

Secret Staircase Books

Shadowed Treasures
Published by Secret Staircase Books, an imprint of
Columbine Publishing Group, LLC
PO Box 416, Angel Fire, NM 87710

Book layout and design by Secret Staircase Books
First trade paperback edition: September, 2022

First e-book edition: September, 2022
* * *
Publisher's Cataloging-in-Publication Data

Morgan, Jennifer J.
Shadowed Treasures/ by Jennifer J. Morgan.
p. cm.
ISBN 978-1649141026 (paperback)
ISBN 978-1649141033 (e-book)

1. Libby Madsen (Fictitious character). 2. Utah—Fiction. 3.
Amateur sleuths—Fiction. 4. Women sleuths—Fiction. I. Title

Libby Madsen Cozy Mystery Series : Book 3.
Morgan, Jennifer J., Libby Madsen cozy mysteries.

BISAC : FICTION / Mystery & Detective.
813/.54

Dedication

This one is for my grandfather.
He was the spunkiest, most adventurous person—right up to
his 95th birthday, which I was fortunate enough to spend with him.
We traveled together several times in recent years (yes, in his 90s)
and I never could keep up with his energy level. He was one of the
most special men in my life and I lost him this year. Thankfully,
before he passed, I was able to spend valuable time with him.
I will treasure that forever. I love you, Grandpa.

CHAPTER ONE

Shadow followed Greg, back and forth, wearing a path between the house and the RV. She knew something was up. The energy was frenetic, but it was a happy sort of vibe. One thing was for certain … as happy as her people were, she was bound to get treats. That had to be the reason she kept following at our heels—like a shadow. The morning mountain air in Heber, Arizona, had a crispness that hadn't been felt yet all summer. It was evident that the seasons were changing, even though the days were still plenty warm. It wasn't unusual for September to have quite hot days, but I loved that the evenings and morning were nice and cool.

"Where did I leave those blankets?" I hollered to Greg from the steps of the RV.

Turning around before heading into the house, he

shrugged. No idea.

I'm beginning to learn that my old ways of throwing a few things in my trusted 4Runner and heading off at a moment's notice were getting a tad more complicated. Two people, twice the planning effort. But, on this trip, Alexis and JJ were joining us, too, so there was even more to consider. Thankfully, we decided not to cram all of us into Greg's RV. JJ and Alexis were renting one of their own.

Greg's arms were loaded as he came up the steps into the RV—a duffle bag of clothes, a tote with Shadow's belongings, another with some of our food items, and the blankets I apparently had left behind in the house. Out of breath, he asked, "What time were they planning to arrive?"

"I believe they'll be here any second. She texted nearly two hours ago, but I'm sure they're being cautious with the mountain roads, as it's their first time."

"Cool, I think these items are the last things from the house." My handsome boyfriend set the bags down on the dining table and headed back outside, Shadow still diligently following her buddy. My heart swelled.

As I stored away the last of our stuff, I heard a vehicle approach and looked outside to see JJ maneuvering their light silver, twenty-foot Class-C motorhome around Greg's circle drive. It was the type with a compartment that hung over the cab of the vehicle—Alexis said there was a bed up there. I couldn't wait to see! I headed over to where they parked about the same time that Shadow came running and barking at our friends. They both hopped out.

"Hey, Shadow, buddy … it's us!" JJ was saying as Shadow seemed unsure about this large thing they had just stepped out of. She had to sniff all around the vehicle before soaking up their love. Even for our tall and muscular friend, this tough detective was a huge softie around children and pets.

"That was so much fun!" Alexis exclaimed as she embraced me. "I can't believe we hadn't tried this before. But, let me tell you, I'm so excited we're getting away now!" She squealed in delight and then turned to Greg and gave him a hug, too.

"Yes, thanks for letting us tag along on this adventure!" JJ reached out to shake Greg's hand. "Good to see you again, man. I think this is just what all of us needed—a break from city life."

No truer words were ever spoken. Since March, our lives have been chaotic—all of ours. First, the pandemic, then assisting with finding a missing girl, and finally, figuring out who was behind several crimes where we live in Mesa, including one where Alexis and her neighbor were attacked. I, for one, am elated to have those days behind us and the bad men safely in jail.

There was good that came from our collective chaos though. First, Isobel (Bella) Crenshaw came into our lives and has become a valued friend and co-worker. Then, JJ solved a decades-old murder investigation and was promoted to detective. Of course, the most important aspect from the last six months for me has been meeting the handsome forest service ranger, Greg Lawson. It feels as though he's always been a part of my life and I count my blessings every day. Still, there are moments that I have a hard time thinking in the terms of 'couple' and struggle occasionally trying to hold onto my independence. Regardless, he has definitely wormed his way into my heart and apparently into my friends' lives as well.

The guys were busy discussing the route we're taking—

Heber to Holbrook, then farther north to Page for the first couple of nights. Then we'd set up a base camp just outside Kanab, Utah, for several days while we rented a Jeep to venture into the national parks—Zion and Bryce—and also, we'd like to check out some of the famed slot canyons. Beyond that, we'd play it by ear for the second week, but we were considering some of the northern communities too, before our time was up. It was an aggressive itinerary considering the fact that this was vacation; however, the four of us are very active hikers so adventures are precisely how we choose to spend our time off.

"Are you guys ready?" I asked, pointing to my watch. "We're burning daylight!"

"Aye, aye!" JJ saluted me. "Let's get on the road!"

Shadow seemed to know this meant the fun was about to start. She spun around, jumped up to high five JJ, and then ran straight toward me as I walked up the steps into Greg's RV. While Greg was doing his final walk around the vehicle, I picked up the hand-held two-way radio and squeezed the button.

"You got a copy, Johnsons?"

Alexis' voice crackled coming through the radio. "10-4! JJ is mimicking Greg outside, it looks like. I've seen them both kicking the tires…"

I laughed. "So happy it worked out to leave Bella in charge of the new therapists for a couple weeks."

"Indeed. Ok, here come the guys … guess we're off!"

The door opened and Greg climbed in, double checking the locks. I added by saying to Alexis, "Safety first—the entire way. Just let us know if we need to slow down a bit … or if you guys need to find a place to pull over. We're in no hurry, just important to get there safely!"

"Roger that! Here's to getting there safely."

I laughed as Greg was buckling his seatbelt. "Alexis is really getting into this, isn't she?"

My smile radiated at Greg. "I'm just so thankful they decided to do this with us. She needed this break more than any one of us. I'm still shocked she left the business!"

"I'm surprised *you* left the spa, honestly."

"Yeah. But the newest therapists from the school have been doing a fantastic job. And, Bella ... talk about a quick learner! She's really got a handle on the business. So, no, I'm fine and promise to relax, let go, and take two weeks off." I gave him a huge smile.

Now, will Alexis and I actually be able to let go and leave work behind? We'll see.

CHAPTER TWO

Our first day traveling was not a long one at all—a mere four-hour drive through the Arizona reservation lands and wide-open vistas. We had called ahead and the Jeep rental company was going to meet us at our campground at the Bullfrog Marina, which is at the north end of Lake Powell. As we pulled into the campground, shortly after two, we found ourselves in awe of the scenic lake view that we'd call home for the first two nights. The lake was shockingly low, but still beautiful. The contrast of the blue water and the surrounding sandstone desert was breathtaking.

Once we were parked, Shadow jumped up to the window and let out a bark. JJ and Alexis were in the site right next to us.

"You probably need a walk, don't you?" I scuffed up

my pup's fur, making her even more excitable. I grabbed her leash, hooked it to her halter—the bra—and off we went. She immediately had her sniffer to the ground, pulling me left, then right. Back and forth, we traversed the short road that led to desert where she was able to finally relieve herself. Once that job was done, she yanked me back toward the road and we walked the long way around while Greg was getting the RV all hooked up to electric, water, and sewer.

Walking around campgrounds was always interesting. I enjoyed seeing different people's setups and the gadgets they have. We passed several people sitting with their dogs in the shade, enjoying a peaceful afternoon at the lake. I forgotten just how much I love being around the water. The sound of motors and children laughing and hollering on the lake echoed far and wide. As we turned with the bend in the road, I noticed an elderly couple ahead who had just finished parking their boat and were unloading. The lady noticed Shadow and immediately came up to us.

"Oh, aren't you the sweetest pup!" she exclaimed as she knelt down to address Shadow. "We lost ours some years ago; I just miss having a dog around." Shadow licked, but managed to control herself and avoided knocking the nice lady over.

"How's the fishing?" I looked over to where the woman's husband was still unloading his tackle.

"Oh. Some days are good—today we didn't catch a thing!" Her energy was warm, but frenetic. She sure was spunky as she told me all about their day out on the lake. Then, very abruptly, "Better get this man his happy hour drink before he gets cranky!" she said with a gravelly texture to her voice. And off she went.

As we walked back to our camp, my thoughts kept

drifting back to the lively lady. They had quite the setup: a Class-C RV which was a little bigger than what the Johnsons had rented, a white Ford pickup truck, and a gray-silver boat which had to be eighteen feet long. That's quite a bit to manage for elderly folks. Well, they appeared to be handling a day out on the lake just fine. I mean, look at them—prioritizing happy hour!

Alexis and JJ already had their camp chairs out, sitting in them with an ice-cold beer, as we walked up to them.

"Well, look at you two … enjoying vacation life, I see!" I turned to my right and saw that Greg was bringing over a couple of chairs and a small ice chest.

"My Lady," he bowed, setting up a chair for me. "And, take your pick…" he opened the ice chest which had an assortment of beer and wine coolers.

"Oooh, look at me getting spoiled!" I reached into the frigid ice and pulled out a refreshing looking peach wine cooler, then gave him a quick kiss. "Thank you!"

Before Greg grabbed his Blue Moon, he put down a small bowl and filled it with water for Shadow. As she drank, we all toasted to our safe arrival at the lake.

* * *

The sun was low on the western horizon when we pulled away from the marina in a rented pontoon. We had decided to put together an assortment of cheese, crackers, fruit, and wine and head out for a private cove to enjoy sunset. It was perfect—the temperature was in the eighties and falling as the sun lowered.

"So, tomorrow we get to play on the lake for the whole day. Then we head to the national parks? Do I have that right?" Alexis smeared more cheese spread onto a cracker as she looked to Greg and JJ for the plan.

Greg glanced at JJ, nodded and then answered, "Yep. We'll go into Page at some point tomorrow also. They have some great restaurants."

"Sounds fantastic. I love that we're spending a quiet evening tonight after all that driving." She took a sip of her wine, then relaxed back in her seat.

Once we had settled in the cove for a while, JJ kept staring at something just up a small ridge from where we were floating.

"What do you see?" I asked.

"I'm not sure, but I'd love to go check it out."

"I'll go with…"

We hopped over the side of the boat, sloshed through the knee-high water trying to keep our sandals from sinking further in the mud. On the shore, we carefully climbed the small hill looking for desert critters with every step we took. It was then that I saw the shiny object he must be after. We climbed the last few feet, then JJ knelt down.

"Someone recently dug here. Look," he said, pointing out the displaced dirt. He picked up an old copper coin his fingers found as he combed through the sand. "Hey, I found a penny!"

I squatted down next to him chanting the old 'find a penny, pick it up…' saying. There was a small rusted metal box that had obviously been pulled out of a hole. It had been cast aside, with its small lid wide open.

Alexis yelled from the boat, "What is it?"

JJ picked up the empty box and held it up. "Just a box. Nothing in it. But, I found a penny!" He held it up.

"Oooh, big find, sweetie!"

We left the box there, in case someone came back for it, and climbed down the hill and back into the boat.

"So, no hidden treasure," Greg said laughing as he helped each of us on board.

"Dangit," I said. "That could have been the treasure that the man from Washington purported to have buried out west somewhere. Remember seeing that online?"

"Oh, yeah, I've read about that. Wasn't it found though?" Alexis asked.

"I think so. But, then again, I haven't kept up on news lately—too much going on." Then I turned to JJ, "Make sure you put that penny in your shoe for good luck…"

"Gonna be hard in flip-flops, but I'll put it in my shorts pocket." He laughed and then looked to the west. "Maybe we should get back? Not sure we should be out in this thing after dark."

Greg nodded his head in agreement. "Yep, let's batten everything down and get going."

As we pulled out of our cove and motored into the larger lake area, another boat was rapidly approaching us. We passed them and waved and that's when I noticed it was the elderly couple I had seen earlier. An eerie feeling came over me.

"Strange," I commented, but not loudly.

"What's that?" my friend asked; she was always so in tune with me.

"Well, when I walked Shadow earlier, I met an elderly couple." I pointed to the boat we had passed. "I think that was them. But, what's strange is how they had just got back from fishing when we stopped to chat. Now they are back in the boat."

"And, that's strange?" Her eyebrows reached upward, questioning.

I shook my head. I couldn't put my finger on it, but something didn't sit well with me.

"They seem pretty old. Are they okay being out at night?"

Alexis laughed. "You seriously worry about *everyone*, don't you? I'm sure they're fine."

She was probably right.

CHAPTER THREE

The next day the four of us spent the entire day out on Lake Powell. We had turned in our pontoon the night before and rented a ski boat, a wake board, and slalom water skis for the day. Greg and JJ had the most fun on the wake board and we pulled them all over the lake. Alexis tried getting up on the skis, but ultimately, she opted to stay onboard being the flag girl while the rest of us played with the toys in the water. It had been years since I had water skied, but once I got up a time or two, it was just like the proverbial 'riding a bike'.

There were several times we took breaks by anchoring in a quiet channel or cove. We'd all dive in the water and Shadow couldn't contain herself any longer. With her life jacket on also, she'd jump in and swim right over to me. She was having the time of her life.

Later that night, we decided to go into Page for dinner. Our hosts at the campground suggested we try the Country BBQ in the center of town; pets welcome. After the long day on the lake, my mouth drooled at the thought of barbeque. During the drive, I just prayed it would be open—it was always a crapshoot with the pandemic closures. We were in luck though, we pulled up and saw their large outdoor seating area.

The waiter who seated us was friendly; he had long brown dreadlocks and an equally long and shaggy beard on his face. My first thought when I saw him was how hot that must be during the summer—all that facial hair. We ordered food and drinks and kicked back, enjoying the cool evening.

Sitting out on the patio under the night sky at a BBQ joint and listening to live country music, I couldn't have been happier. The place was not super crowded, and the tables were set a good distance apart. I suppose this was why the place was allowed to have the 'dine-in' option. The best part was that it was a dog-friendly patio so Shadow rested right at my feet. She was completely tuckered out after the day on the lake.

As I was listening to the cover band play a Johnny Cash song, Shadow got up and I saw what she was interested in. She eyed an elderly couple who made their way around the tables and to some floor space closer to the band. Her tail started to wag, slapping the side of my sunburned legs. Hmm, it was the same couple from the campground. Facing each other, they took each other's hands, and started dancing. I couldn't help but admire their energy—they were remarkable!

"Hey, look…" I pointed out to Alexis.

"Aren't they cute!" her hand went to cover her mouth as she giggled.

"Those are the two in the boat from that cove yesterday."

"Nuh-uh. They're *old*."

"I know! That's why I was worried last night."

"Well, look at them. They made it out alive *and* they're here dancing tonight. Awwwww…"

We all were transfixed by the cute couple. She was short and stout—maybe five foot one. He was tall and thin—I would guess six feet tall. Her platinum blonde hair was fixed just so with its curls and a bit of feathering to it, too. He had very white-silver straight hair, perfectly combed in place. He twirled her around and they stepped right back into the beat, never taking their eyes off each other. The music stopped and they passed right by our table when the lady stopped.

"Heyyyy! You're the dog lady!" she shouted, then turned to her partner. "Honey, this is the one with the black Lab." Then Shadow rubbed up against her leg. "Oh, hey, right here … look, what a sweet dog!" She bent down and petted Shadow as she wriggled about.

He turned to me and reached out to shake my hand. I couldn't help but stare into his crystal blue eyes as he grabbed my hand. He was handsome—I think back in the day, you'd say *debonair;* he was that striking. "Hi! Pleasure to meet you. Agatha has been going on about that dog of yours," he said sweetly.

"Oh, nice to meet you, too." I looked over my shoulder and added, "This is my boyfriend, Greg." He stood and shook the man's hand, and then Agatha's. "And these are my good friends, JJ and Alexis." They both stood and greeted each of them.

"I'm Eugene," the silver fox greeted. "And this here is Agatha."

Greg ushered them over, offering for them to join us just as the band was getting ready to take a break. The couple retrieved their drinks from their table and accepted our offer.

"So, Eugene, what brings you to Lake Powell?" JJ asked.

"Son, we travel all over. We're from Colorado; just got done with a big hunt."

The men hunkered down at one end of the table exchanging hunting stories. JJ and Greg were in their element. At the girls' end of the table, Agatha was full of her own tales.

"I saw you guys back out on the lake last night. When we passed you going into that cove," I reminded.

"That's right. Well, you have to hear *this* story … we got back in there, pulled up to the shore, and then got stuck. The engine died! Yep, you heard correct—it just died." Her animation was cracking us up, but I sensed it really wasn't supposed to be a funny story. "Eugene said, 'hop out and take this rope' … so *I did!*" Her eyes were huge and her mouth started to contort. "Oh, and let me tell ya, that water was *cold*. But, I got out, grabbed the rope he threw to me. Then, he says 'tie it around your waist'!" She looked over to her right, to see if he was listening. "I was thinking, what was the old bat going to do—drown me right here?!"

My thoughts exactly, except they were both sitting with us, so we knew the outcome must have been okay. I got such a kick out of her storytelling—my guess was she could be Italian. I could picture her whole family together, talking loudly, and gesticulating wildly. Really nice lady, but her only volume was *high*. When I looked over at Eugene, he spoke quietly—all the men leaned in to hear.

She continued, "Oh, no … you just wait! It gets better! I tied the rope and then *pulled the damn boat away from shore!!* That's when we learned the engine was dead. We were stuck anyway!"

Alexis' eyes were wide, her hand to her mouth. "How did you get out?"

"Well, that's just it—we didn't!" Her eyes widened and the pace of her speech quickened. "We slept on the boat! It was *freezing* overnight. I didn't have a change of clothes, no blanket. I've never been so cold in my life. But, Eugene … well, that man doesn't let anything get him flustered. Nope. We just cuddled and hunkered down. Early in the morning, the deputies came and found us. It was so sweet. Our neighbors—you know, right there in that campground we're all in—they realized we hadn't come back so they called for help. They were worried about us!"

"Why did you go there at night?" I asked.

"Oh, Eugene. He loves night fishing. Plus, he's always on the hunt for a treasure."

"A treasure?" Alexis asked. "What kind of treasure?"

"Oh, I don't know. I just go along for the ride. What else are you going to do when you're our age?"

Chuckling on the inside, I found this little lady so amusing. I wanted so much to ask their ages, but that's rude so I didn't. She went on and on until the band started up again. As soon as Willie Nelson's *On The Road Again* sounded, she jumped up.

"Honey, *they're playing our song!*" she yelled out to

Eugene. He promptly got up and they shuffled back onto the dance floor.

Greg moved closer to me again. "That man is amazing! Did you know he is 95?"

My jaw dropped. I knew they were older, but never in my wildest dream had I imagined *that old*. "Look at them! And I'm about dead after one day on the lake. Did he indicate how old she is?"

"Think he said she's turning 85 later this month. And, get this … they just spent two *weeks* out in the Colorado mountains hunting elk. Yes, *both of them*. She hunts too!"

"Wow, that's remarkable." As interesting as it was, I couldn't hold my yawn back. "This 38-year-old is very tired and needs some sleep." My eyes felt like lead weights. A full day in the sun and now a couple drinks too; I was spent. We looked over to Alexis and JJ and we all exchanged the look that meant, we've got to call it a night.

We left Eugene and Agatha dancing the night away.

CHAPTER FOUR

I couldn't help but sing *On The Road Again* into the two-way radio as our group pulled out of the campground to make the short journey over to Kanab, Utah, the next morning. We all had commented what a fun time we had in Page the night before. The images of our newfound friends dancing, telling their tales, and the ear worm still lingering with country music tunes made me smile. I couldn't help but be appreciative of such a perfect vacation getaway. It was so needed after several months of stress.

"Where are we staying in Kanab? I know you told me when you made the arrangements," I asked Greg, once we were farther down Hwy 89.

"I have the name of it written down on that notepad over there, can't remember it." He pointed to the pad of paper. "But, I remember it sounded so cool. It's just outside of the town of Kanab. They restrict use of light at night so that all campers can enjoy the dark skies. I even brought my telescope, hoping we'll get to see the Milky Way." His kid-like excitement was infectious.

"That sounds amazing."

We had decided last night to get an early start this morning. Then we could get set up at the campground, retrieve our four-wheeling excursion vehicle from the camp hosts, and still have the whole day to play. Thankfully, the camp hosts were accommodating for our early arrival.

* * *

Alexis put together a beautiful salad and I brought some sushi we had picked up from the market in Page. We sat around at our friend's campsite and enjoyed lunch before setting out for a hike. The weather was perfect on the late September day—the highs were only expected to be in the 80s and there was a light cloud covering too.

"I think that's our four-wheeling vehicle right there," I pointed to a camouflage green Jeep-like vehicle coming up the lane.

"Yep, that's our Roxor!" Greg exclaimed.

Alexis furrowed her brows. "I've never heard of that. Looks like a Jeep?"

JJ's eyes lit up. "It is similar to a Jeep for four wheeling purposes. It's just the older style called a Mahindra Roxor. Back in the '40s I think there were Willys and then somewhere around the '60s, you had the Jeep CJ. This is a cross between those. They're cool!"

Greg and JJ got up to greet our camp host who had just brought it over. The men were in hog heaven, drooling over the machinery. They circled the vehicle, admiring all the features, and then all three men's heads disappeared as they looked under the hood.

"It doesn't take much to keep them happy and entertained, does it?" Alexis asked, smiling as she observed her husband.

I just smiled and nodded. I was thrilled at how well the guys got along. They both were easygoing men who had similar interests. That made a trip like this one so much easier—everyone got along.

We watched the guys hop in with the camp host to take a practice run around the campground, and learn the features of the rental. Since we were all done eating, we decided we had better clean up to be ready to go when they returned. We knew just how excited they would be to get out on this adventure. We were excited, too!

Our camp hosts, Andrew and Leslie Mann, were incredible. We told them the type of excursions we'd like to experience in Utah and they planned out a custom itinerary just for our group. We were staying at their campground for several nights so they certainly had their hands full in planning our getaways. Today, the plan was to head out to White Pocket, which was technically the direction we just came from, in Arizona—but right near the border of Utah. Andrew explained that while the road was open to the public, it was highly recommended only for high clearance vehicles. Many people apparently ignored that warning; Andrew detailed several rescue operations he'd been involved in using the Roxor.

We packed up extra food and water into the small ice chest. For safety's sake, I grabbed the first aid kit, a few blankets, and we added some extra layers of clothing in our backpacks. Where we were going was far off the beaten path and after hearing how many people had gotten stranded, well, one could never be overly prepared, right?

It wasn't long before Shadow was loaded into her spot, we all fastened our seatbelts, and then we were off. Andrew had provided us a handheld GPS unit with the route already programmed in. It would take us a couple hours each way, plus time for hiking around the beautiful rock formations once we were there. I figured, more than likely, we wouldn't be back until after dark.

About an hour into the journey, I couldn't contain my smile as we all bounced along slowly on the deeply-rutted, long, dusty road. It felt so good to be away from the city, with no cares in the world. So far, we had not encountered any other explorers. We were deep within the remote Vermilion Cliffs National Monument—miles from civilization. I looked back at my friends, who sandwiched Shadow in the backseat—everyone was getting jostled around, but it looked like they were enjoying themselves. Even in the enclosed vehicle, we didn't try to talk over the engine and wind noise.

After a long stretch of fighting through deep sand, we pulled up to the White Pocket trailhead sign. Greg turned off the engine, with that adolescent boy's smile, which indicated that was the coolest thing he's done in a long time. I wondered with the sudden silence whether I had gone deaf. It got so quiet. Then, JJ spoke up.

"I can see why Andrew recommended a four-wheel drive," he said, looking back toward the trail we had traversed. "Those ruts were something. Couldn't imagine going through that during monsoons."

Alexis brushed off some dust, and tied on a head scarf to shield her scalp from the sun. "That was cool though!" She turned and pointed to the gorgeous sandstone formation in front of us. "But this is what I'm here for … can't wait to hike up that!"

Shadow was also more than eager to get moving as well. We loaded some water bottles into our backpacks and then headed out—Greg led the way, with Shadow and JJ bringing up the rear.

"I'm surprised no one else is here," JJ said.

"Maybe morning was busier? It's getting late in the day now," I said.

We followed the trail, which took us along the waves of the formation, through a group of domes and ridges, and then finally to the top of a slope where we could see down onto the mesa below.

"Andrew was correct," Greg took a sip of his water, "this is just as beautiful as The Wave, and without having to wait for the permit."

"I've heard many are unable to get that permit," I added. "But, you are right … this is gorgeous. And, I'm happy we have the place to ourselves." Greg put his arm around me. I turned to him for a kiss.

Lexi was taking pictures. Shadow was sniffing everywhere. JJ continued around the next bluff, just out of our sight. It was perfect here; I wished we had brought tents for overnight. I could just imagine seeing the Milky Way this far from the city.

"Hey guys! C'mere," JJ yelled.

Shadow was the first to take off in the direction of JJ's voice, then we all followed.

"Look—there in the distance," he pointed toward

another formation at a lower elevation "Is that part of this Paria Plateau, do you suppose?"

Greg grabbed the binoculars from his pack. Taking off his aviators, he squinted. He pulled back from the spectacles, searching for the object, then trying again to line it all up. "That ... isn't part of nature. It looks like something manmade. Here, take a look." He handed the binoculars over to JJ.

"Ah, yeah ... that's weird. Out of place."

"I wanna see!" I piped up. JJ handed them over.

"Guys. I think it's a ... a, shoot, what do you call those things? *A monolith*?" Well, that's a very strange thing to find out here in the desert, I thought.

We had to get a closer look so we climbed down off the formation and started the half-mile journey to check out the shiny metal structure. It was huge—at least ten to twelve feet tall. Once we were physically touching it, we could see that it was a solid metallic structure seemingly on a firm foundation. We couldn't budge it. All four of us continued to circle the ten-foot diameter desert oddity. How did it get here? Or more importantly, *why is it here?*

JJ bent down. "Hmmm. What's this? Look—this side doesn't appear to be one solid piece." He began to pry at a spot near the base, then searched the area for a stick or flat rock.

I took off my sunglasses and knelt down near JJ. He was right. Along one edge it appeared to be a seam with a jagged edge to it. I stood up to let Greg get a closer look.

"Is there an opening?" Greg inquired.

JJ found a small, but flat rock and knelt down onto the ground. "It could be," he groaned as he tried to get the makeshift tool to work for him. He worked at it for a few minutes before a small piece gave way. Using his hands now, he pried until a small portion of the metal opened up and fell into his hands. "Gotta flashlight in your pack, Greg?"

"Yep, right here." Greg handed the light over.

Alexis and I stood to the side, watching the guys hunker down over the small opening. JJ reached inside and when he pulled his hand out, he brought out a small green felt pouch. I got excited and wanted to see what was in there. I held my hand out and JJ placed it in my palm. Everyone watched as I opened the drawstrings and poured out the contents into the bowl Greg made with his hands.

Our eyes were wide with anticipation.

Then, we just laughed as we stared into Greg's palms. There were two very tiny rocks—one was quite blue, perhaps it was turquoise. Then, there was the wadded-up piece of paper.

CHAPTER FIVE

We arrived back at the campground around seven that evening. It was dark, but Andrew saw us pulling in and met us at the drop-off point.

"How was it?" he asked, smiling.

"Oh man, this vehicle is amazing!" Greg exclaimed.

"Thank you for the recommendation ... you were right, way better than waiting on a permit for The Wave," Alexis added.

I was still confused as to why the Bureau of Land Management would place a monolith out there. Everyone else seemed to have forgotten about what we found. "Why is there a monolith out there in the desert?" I asked Andrew.

His head tilted and eyes squinted. "Monolith?"

JJ started describing the metallic structure we saw maybe half a mile from the White Pocket southernmost formation. Andrew knew nothing about it and quite frankly, it was obvious he didn't believe us. It didn't matter to me one way or another, I just wondered why something so unnatural was constructed on the sacred Navajo land. Who would allow that?

Our attention was diverted when Andrew's wife, Leslie, walked up. "Howdy, folks!" She pointed over to a pavilion structure at the northwest corner of the property where a small group had assembled by a nice roaring fire. "Feel free to join us on our terrace … bring your drink of choice, and you'll find a small spread of appetizers to enjoy."

We all looked to one another and agreed that sounded like fun. Shadow was laying at my feet, obviously tired from a big day out.

I looked to Greg, "Shall we put our stuff in the RV? I'll feed Shadow and leave her to rest."

"Sounds like a plan."

The group around the fire quietly conversed to the background music—a gentleman off to one side, strumming on his guitar. Our group of four chose one of the picnic tables to sit at while we enjoyed some cheese and crackers.

Greg held up his Blue Moon, "To a great day of exploring!" JJ lifted his beer; Alexis and I cheered with our glasses of Cabernet. A little quieter he added, "And, to our great *treasure*…"

JJ's eyes looked over to me. "Do you still have that note we found in there?"

"Yep!" I dug it out from my shorts pocket and unfolded the small piece of paper with a symbol of a fish drawn on it.

"Read it again…" JJ said, just like a kid at bedtime.

"All it says is: *CLS*" At least I think those were the letters. It was faded and worn so it was difficult to tell.

"And, what else was in that compartment?" Alexis asked.

JJ spoke up, "Just the rocks and that note. That's it."

"Woo-hoo! Big *treasure* we found!" I celebrated by lifting my glass again. Everyone's eyes rolled and we all took another sip as a toast, laughing. I wadded up the paper and put it back into my pocket before asking, "What's on the agenda for tomorrow?"

Greg was happy to report, "Tomorrow, we head to Zion National Park. Andrew has arranged another rental for us—this time a Jeep Wrangler—to be delivered to us in the morning. We'll actually be keeping it the rest of the time we're in Utah. As soon as it's delivered, then we'll head out for some more hiking. I hear the park is amazing."

We all turned when we heard a familiar voice.

"Well, I thought that was you guys…" Agatha walked up behind me and grabbed my shoulder, startling me. "Eugene said I was crazy, but I just knew I recognized you. How're y'all doin'?"

Greg and JJ stood up and greeted Agatha. Alexis and I glanced over at each other—evidently, we were both wondering what the odds were of running into this couple again. Eugene walked up then.

"Hey … Agatha was right." His smile was infectious and he exuded kindness. "Are you following us?" he teased. We all laughed.

"Hello, sir!" Greg greeted Eugene with a firm handshake. "Good to see you again. Come on over …

there's plenty of room here."

We all scootched down and made room for the elderly pair.

JJ asked, "What brings you to Kanab? Headed to the National Parks?"

Both Agatha and Eugene winced, looked at each other, then back at JJ. "We're just roaming around. We have lots of family to visit and we just stay on the go," he laughed, seemingly staying vague with his answer.

Agatha cut in, "You know, at our age … it's best we just stay on the move. Plus, you can't slow this guy down." She pointed at her husband. "If he's not seeking a new adventure, he'll just get cranky. He doesn't like to sit still."

I caught another look exchanged between the two. There was something about this pair, but I just couldn't place it so I sat back, watching the group interact. Greg was describing our trip out to White Pocket and Eugene was captivated by the whole story … the Roxor, the sandstone formations, and then the story of finding a pouch in the monolith. Eugene was particularly interested in the adventure and the men continued their conversation in quieter tones at their end of the table.

Agatha was explaining to Alexis and me that they left Lake Powell in the afternoon after spending all morning fishing. The boat was working fine after a guy there at the marina replaced a fuse … but she was still concerned about going too far and getting stuck again.

"Eugene doesn't worry about that kind of thing at all. And, he trusts … how does he know whether that guy actually fixed the problem? Oh, no, he doesn't even question it—just takes off for the other side of the lake with no concern at all." She shook her head, looking down.

"Anyway, that's why we stopped here. We were supposed to make it to Cedar City today, but we didn't even leave Lake Powell until after four!"

"Oh, so you have family in Cedar City?" I asked.

"Yep, he has cousins everywhere…"

Eugene obviously heard what she what telling us. "Agatha, I told you we don't discuss our plans with anyone." His voice was calm, but the inference was pointed.

Agatha hung her head a bit, took her toothpick she'd been gnawing on, and started digging deeper into those teeth. Her eyebrows furrowed, she said in a low voice, "I'm ready for bed." She didn't wait for Eugene, she got up and shuffled out into the darkness.

"Sorry 'bout her, she can talk for days." Eugene made no move to join his wife. Instead, he grabbed another beer and listened to Greg talk about the recent fires in Arizona.

Alexis and I poured some more wine and enjoyed the guitar music. The small fire glowed, with an occasional spark that caught our eyes. I looked up and it appeared the stars were dancing just above my head among an ink-black canvas.

"Got a text from Bella earlier," Alexis started, then took a sip of her wine. "She's talking about heading down to Patagonia on her days off this weekend. Remember, that's where that meditation retreat relocated a couple years back?"

"Oh, yeah … isn't that where you went for your certification when they were in Tucson? Sounds like she must have really enjoyed the meditation work the two of you have been doing, to want to go down to Patagonia."

She nodded. "It seems so. Hopefully, this is something she really wants to do and she's not just trying to please me. I think it could be great for her—part of healing those childhood traumas."

"When does her EMT course end?"

"Not sure, but I know she has a break during October. If I remember right, she doesn't get certified until early next year."

Eugene stood up, came over to us girls and bade us goodnight with a pat on our shoulders. Once he was gone, JJ and Greg moved over closer to us.

"My mind is blown with everything that ninety-five-year-old has done," JJ stated.

Greg added, "But, how do you *really* think they're managing on this trip? Do you truly believe they've done all they've said they have?" He swallowed his sip of beer, and looked over at me, smiling. "I'm not sure what to believe. They are quite the couple though, huh?"

"What makes you say that?" I was curious.

"Oh, they just have some wild tales." Greg laughed.

"Makes me think of the stereotypical 'fish story' when he gets into the storytelling." JJ chuckled, nearly choking on his sip of beer. "There's something about Eugene though that is so familiar. Like we've met somewhere before. It's strange, but after only a couple of conversations, I feel oddly connected to him."

Alexis turned to JJ, puzzled, and then said, "I don't think we've met them before. However, there's something secretive and the way he shushed her before she headed off. I thought they were going to get into a thing there. It's weird, right?"

"Yesss!" we all agreed at once.

"Well, they are very nice. I admire how they are still out doing what they do at their age. It's none of our business what they're up to or how they manage it. I'm just glad we've met them." I yawned, then looked to Greg. "Ready to hit it? We have a big day tomorrow."

Everyone agreed and we said goodnight to our camp hosts, then decided to stroll the long way back to our sites. Farther away from the fire, our eyes adjusted to the darkness. We found a nice area near the dog park at the far end of the camp where there were several hammocks set up. Greg and I climbed into one; Alexis and JJ into another. Lying there swinging, each of us marveled at the bright, distinct galaxy suspended above. The silence was a nice respite from an active day filled with exploration. Crickets chirped. I closed my eyes, imagining that we were all alone. The swinging hammocks made a slight whooshing sound, which seemed to lull us further into the stars above.

A coyote howled in the distance.

We kept swinging; no one spoke.

There was a winged creature that flew low overhead— an owl?

Everything was silent. Greg was perfectly still, and I heard nothing from my friends either. My thoughts were drifting away.

More coyotes howling…

It was the perfect desert night, not too hot or cold. My mind drifted again, thinking how quiet all the campers were. Didn't sound like anyone was around—and, as soon as that thought occurred, I startled. An engine fired up. I rolled my head north, looking toward the sound.

Where on earth are Eugene and Agatha going this late at night?

CHAPTER SIX

I accidentally tipped us over in the hammock trying to see if that really was their pickup leaving. Greg was sprawled out on top of me when we landed the couple feet onto the ground. Clambering to get up, and trying to catch my breath, I clawed my way out from under him. Groaning to turn over, I got on all fours, then stood up. Alexis and JJ were already out of their hammock.

"Isn't that..." Alexis started to question.

"Yeah, that's what I was thinking..." I finished her thought.

We all watched the tail lights as the Walkers pulled out of the campground. I looked all around—apparently, we had been in the hammocks longer than I'd thought. The group at the terrace had dismantled and the fire was out. Then, once the diesel was out of the park, it was silent again.

The next morning, our Jeep Wrangler was delivered promptly at eight o'clock, exactly as promised. We had just finished breakfast—Alexis and I went all out—eggs, turkey sausage, pancakes, and mixed berries. That carb load and protein would get us through the day's rigorous hike. As soon as we cleaned up, we loaded the Jeep with our backpacks and all the provisions for our journey.

The drive to Zion National from Kanab took us approximately forty-five minutes. After paying our park entrance fees, we drove straight to the Weeping Rock trailhead, which was the access point to the East Rim Trail. It would take us approximately six hours to hike the eight-mile loop once we branched off to The Observation Point trail a few miles into the hike. We had planned for eight hours *just in case*.

Shadow bounded out of the Jeep and immediately started yipping excitedly. She apparently slept great last night and was raring to go again today. I wished I could say the same. It had taken me a long time to fall asleep, wondering if Eugene and Agatha were okay. I finally convinced myself that worrying about them was not helpful at all. After all, they weren't my family. We'd literally just met them the day before and here I was, sleepless with worry. I just needed to let it go.

About two hours into our hike, we were over four miles along on the trail, which was the easiest part. We all seemed to be enjoying the scenery and chatting away. I knew the hard part was near; we'd need all our strength for the two-thousand-foot elevation change. Since I was in the lead, I began to set that pace.

"Hey, why're we slowing…" Greg complained.

"Just wait. You'll see," I smiled, already breathing heavily.

JJ fell right in line with the new pace. Alexis was looking ahead. "Hey, is that the trail high up on that ridge over there?" she asked.

"Yep, that's where we're headed." I looked back at her and saw her eyes get huge.

Around the next corner, the terrain turned rocky and we started climbing. Our pace slowed. Our breathing became rapid. The trail turned abruptly and we proceeded up the next switchback. About a quarter mile later, there was a nice outcropping of trees producing shade. Shadow and I stopped and waited for the three to catch up. I poured some water for Shadow and she laid down.

"You… ugh… you, weren't kidding," Greg said completely out of breath and removing his water bottle from his belt. "When does it level off again?"

Alexis pointed upward again. "Clearly, not for a while."

I pulled out my trail map. "It looks like we still have a couple more miles upward before it levels, then we head downhill around the loop until we end up back at the trailhead. We've got a ways to go!" I took a nice long pull on my water bottle, then offered Shadow a couple treats, before checking in with the group. "Is everybody doing okay?"

JJ already looked refreshed. "Let's do it!" Alexis and Greg took a couple deeper breaths and then agreed with equal enthusiasm

"Alright, let's get going … there's a lot of this trail left to explore." I continued to lead the way.

By the time we had made our way around the loop and were on our last mile, it was clear that this group was spent. Shadow's tongue drooped from her mouth for the last two miles. We stopped several times to cool down and hydrate. The day wasn't hot by any means, but the exertion was intense.

When we got to the vehicle, Greg opened the back of the Jeep to remove the ice chest, which held another stash of cold drinks for everyone. We all collapsed to the ground, pulling off our hiking boots, soaking wet socks, and replacing them with sandals. I poured some water over my head and also made sure Shadow got more to drink. She was panting hard, but the look on her face spoke volumes. If she could talk, I would imagine she was saying "what a perfect day!" After thirty minutes or so, we had cooled down and been off our feet long enough where we could consider getting up again.

JJ's eyes lit up. "Hey, wanna hit that microbrew place we saw in Kanab on the way back? I could use a cheeseburger and a beer right about now!"

"Hell yeah," Greg agreed.

"Nothing sounds better … great idea!" Alexis and I were all in.

We grudgingly stood, loaded our packs into the Jeep, and then headed out of Zion National Park. Thirty minutes later, we pulled up to the Southwest Microbrew, only to learn there was no dine-in option; they were only offering pickup service. We convinced ourselves that was okay since the campground wasn't far. We placed our to-go order—gouda and bacon cheeseburgers, truffle fries, and two growlers of their craft brew. Alexis and I were interested in their apricot ale and the guys wanted the award-winning IPA. The aroma for the rest of our car ride was excruciating for us all. Even though we weren't starving when we ordered, by the time we pulled up at the campground, we were ravenous.

The sun had settled behind distant hills as we sat silently devouring the most scrumptious cheeseburgers any of us had ever eaten. I took one sip of Greg's IPA and knew immediately that Alexis and I made the right decision on the light-colored, very slight tinge of sweet, ice-cold apricot pale ale. IPAs were bitter tasting to me, but JJ and Greg loved the beer. I'm not sure—it could have been the ten-mile aggressive hike, or the best burgers and fries I've had—but I agreed with Shadow, today *was* perfect.

Andrew pulled up on his side-by-side just as we were cleaning up from dinner. "Hey, how was Zion?" he asked.

"Great, thanks! Oh man, that trail you suggested was amazing," Greg gushed. "And, I'm sure you've been to Southwest Microbrew?"

"Oh yeah, did you get the gouda burger?"

Greg's eyes rolled back in his head, his hands straight to his belly. "*That* was fantastic!" All of us were nodding in agreement with equal looks of contentment. "Hey man, come join us…" he lifted the growler, "we got that famous IPA."

"Cool … thanks," he turned off his vehicle and joined us. JJ grabbed a glass and poured him a beer.

Alexis turned to Andrew, "Hey, the older couple…" her eyes looked to the campsite to the south of us.

"Ah, yeah, they came back this afternoon. I still don't know why they left so late last night. I mean, *I* don't even like driving at night."

"That's what we were thinking," JJ said, then looked

skeptically toward Alexis.

"What?" asked Andrew. "Seems like there's more to the story…"

JJ just nodded slightly. "I don't know, man, but it's strange. We first ran into them in Page … Lake Powell, before we arrived here. Had fun at a BBQ joint listening to music and also heard a bunch of the ol' man's stories. Then last night, on your terrace, they were very nice as well. But, in the end, there was something … well, *secretive* going on between them…" he looked again to Alexis.

She picked up where JJ left off. "Yeah, I thought about that, too. For instance, his wife was irritated with him when he scolded her … you know, when we were sitting by the fire. She was just talking about their day at the lake. She stomped off, then after he'd joined her awhile later … well, that's when we saw them leave the campground. I just hope there's nothing serious going on."

Andrew nodded and took a sip of his beer. "I don't know. I haven't talked with them since they've been here, but they sure seem social. Guess every couple has their…" his voice turned to a whisper and he leaned in … "Actually, here they come now." He tilted his head slightly in their direction.

"Well, hi there, Eugene, Agatha … please, come join us!" I stood up and walked toward the two. Shadow beat me to it, but thankfully she didn't jump up on them. Eugene and Agatha both reached down to pet her and then they proceeded to give me a giant hug.

"Hello there! Looks like a party over here … we can't resist a party!" the crystal blue-eyed gentleman smiled. "I don't think we've met…" he held out his hand to Andrew who introduced himself. "Oh, oh yeah, that's right, we met your wife yesterday. Leanne ... no, Leslie, right?"

"That's right. Well, come have a seat." They both sat at the campground-provided picnic table. Shadow moved right in and sat on Eugene's feet. Her loving gaze at this elderly man was heartwarming. She was so drawn to him.

Maybe we should have ordered another jug of beer, I thought as they settled in ... but as it turned out, they weren't interested in beer anyway. After topping the rest of us off, I dived right in to where no one else was willing to go.

"So, Eugene, where did you head off to in the night?"

He squirmed in his seat and looked over to Agatha next to him. "Oh, you know ..." he shifted around and changed the subject abruptly. "This is a really nice rig you've got here, Greg."

We glanced around at one another. He flat-out ignored my question!

Greg thanked him for the RV compliment.

"What time did you get back?" I asked, hoping to use a different angle to get them talking. I noticed Agatha stayed quiet; she just stared at the ground while Eugene did the talking.

"Oh, sometime before lunch," he answered. "You guys weren't around. Where'd you all go anyway?"

Apparently, we weren't going to get any further details so we filled them in on our day's adventures instead. Andrew bowed out after about fifteen minutes—it was getting dark out and he needed to tend to the fire on the terrace for the other guests. He had already given Greg all the details for tomorrow's outing; we were scheduled to do a shorter, slot canyon venture with a guide.

I, for one, was exhausted. Shadow seconded that

motion, and Greg was yawning consistently while being polite, listening to Eugene's tales. They finally got the hint, and once they said farewell, we watched them venture over to join the others on the terrace.

Where do those two get their energy? They were literally out all night!

CHAPTER SEVEN

We were all on our own for breakfast and had agreed to meet up when the outfitter's van was due to arrive at 9 a.m. Greg and I enjoyed coffee and oatmeal.

"Where are those power bars? We're going to need a little something later on. Maybe some fruit too?" I suggested.

"Sounds good. Look right up there—second cabinet over," he pointed across from where I stood.

I re-packed our backpacks with all the essentials, then headed outside to get some stretching done before the guides arrived. I noticed as I stepped out and looked across the way that Eugene's pickup was gone again. Those two sure stayed on the move.

Alexis was already on her yoga mat and halfway through her workout. I headed over to their site next door and set my mat right next to hers on the flat dirt surface.

"Good morning!" she said quietly as she moved into downward dog.

"It's actually slightly chilly this morning, isn't it?" I laid down on my back, pulled my knees to my chest and gently rocked back and forth. "Ugh, this ground is hard!"

"It's gorgeous out. I sure could get used to vacation!" Lexi stood into a sun salutation, then went gently down to the mat holding a plank, and eventually, back into downward dog again, repeating the flow.

"How's Joshua doing without you guys?"

"Oh, he looked great when we video chatted last night. He *loves* JJ's mother. She spoils him rotten!"

I sat up, crossed my legs, and slowly began making circles with my torso—stretching my lower back, abs, and hips. "I hope Bella is hanging in there at the spa. Probably should call."

"Oh, completely forgot to tell you! I did touch base with her yesterday morning before we left. They're doing fine." She reached up, stretching high above her head again, then down to the ground completing the flow.

"Oh right. You didn't forget—I did. I think you told me yesterday that she's headed back to the meditation retreat this weekend, right?"

"Yes! I'm so proud," she smiled. "I think it's a perfect complement to her therapy. Now, to get *you* meditating more regularly."

"I know, I know. I'll get better at it."

"Consistency. That's all."

I began my morning flow sequence with many grunts and groans. My legs ached. My back was stiff. Exactly why I needed yoga this morning. Alexis started earlier than me, so perhaps she was already warmed up—but there were no agonizing sounds coming from her.

"You don't worry about how easily she seems to follow others?" I asked.

"No. Why?"

"Oh, nothing. I think I've just become protective of her ever since she moved in with me."

"I could see that. No, I think she's handling everything very well. EMT training, working full-time, and now therapy and meditation. She's recovering well."

Thirty minutes later, we rolled up our mats. It wasn't ten minutes after that when the outfitter van pulled into the campground. All of us dressed in variations of lightweight long-sleeved hiking shirts in bright colors; the guys wore pants and us girls were in shorts. We quickly gathered our packs, locked up, loaded into the van, and we were off.

The sun shone bright and the day was beginning to warm up. We hiked along a sandy, dry wash for a couple of miles until we came to the rock formations. The colors were brilliant—yellow, coral, brown, and almost pink in some places. It took my breath away when I attempted to look upward at the majestically tall sandstone and limestone walls. The sheer, steep canyon walls appeared to ascend into heaven. The passageways became narrow, with slats of sunlight sneaking through at varying points. The temperature dropped dramatically once we were strolling along between the stone crevices.

Shadow followed at the heels of our guides—Kyle and Marley. Periodically, they stopped and filled us in on the history of the area. Shadow would sit, looking up at them, appearing to be just as interested as we were. Kyle was very knowledgeable about the area; he was a college graduate with an emphasis in archaeology from the University of Utah. The brown-haired, tanned, and overall good-looking kid said he'd been working for the outfitter company for the past four years while completing college. He had ambitions of completing his masters' studies in glacial geology. Already, I had learned more than I probably ever needed to know about erosion and how the sandstone formations continuously change. I found them beautiful and I loved the exercise we were getting while exploring, but I'd never remember the science behind it all. Thank goodness for these graduates, paying attention to climate change—Kyle was very passionate about the rocks.

Marley had been introduced as a first-time intern with the company. He was quiet and let Kyle do most of the talking. I found myself staring at him throughout the day. He seemed very familiar to me. He wasn't young like Kyle; he appeared to be older than anyone in our group actually. With his French Foreign Legion-looking desert hat and wrap-around dark sunglasses, it was difficult to see his features. He had dreadlocks—braids that were pulled back into a thick ponytail, flowing well past the sun cape of his hat and down to the middle of his back. His tall lithe frame was covered by his light colored long-sleeved shirt and hiking pants. *Seems like we've seen him somewhere before.*

We stopped for a rest and broke out the water and fruit.

Greg carefully peeled his orange, putting the peelings back into his backpack. "Marley, do you work only for this outfitter, or for multiple? It seems like we've seen you around the area before today."

Ah, ha! I wasn't the only one who had picked up on this.

Marley sucked down water before he answered.

Twisting the cap back on his insulated water bottle, he said succinctly, "I have worked several odd jobs in the region." He stared at the ground, not making eye contact, and he didn't elaborate.

"Cool. Anywhere we may have met you previously?" Greg prodded.

"Nah."

The glance that Greg and I exchanged told me he wanted to learn more. I knew something was familiar, and Greg was sure of it, too. But, one thing that was also sure, this guy was not the talkative type, so this conversation was done.

We continued along for a couple more miles, exploring the slot canyon and climbing up the rocky terrain to get back to where we had started. JJ and I hung back from the group a bit.

"You'd think for a guide, he'd be a little more personable," JJ whispered to me. "Maybe this isn't his day job? Just getting a few bucks on the side … doesn't feel he has to be nice?"

I snorted, laughing, then realized I'd caught the attention of the group ahead. "Sorry!" I yelled out. Then, turned back to JJ whispering, "Strange indeed."

"I guess no stranger than anyone else we've met on this trip."

I laughed out loud again. "No kidding. I've really enjoyed meeting new people, but sheesh. Eugene and Agatha are a hoot, though, huh?"

"I just can't shake the feeling that I know Eugene from somewhere." JJ shook his head. "Does he seem familiar to you?"

"Nah."

"That's what Alexis says too. I must be imagining it. I'm sure there's someone I met along the way that resembles him somehow. I just can't place it though."

We picked up our pace, walking along with the rest of the group again. The scenery was amazing. Who knew the desert could be this gorgeous, but it really was. None of us were ready for our hike to end after the five miles, but we sure were looking forward to an ice-cold beer, guacamole, chips and salsa when we returned to our campground.

CHAPTER EIGHT

Agatha came running the second she saw us pull up. She was frantic.

"He's gone! He just left me here!" she was screaming and waving a piece of paper in my face as I met her in the roadway between our two camps. Alexis, JJ, and Greg followed me.

"What do you mean he left you?" I took the paper and tried to read. She kept shouting, but Shadow tried to distract her by jumping up for a kiss. It worked. The note just said: I'll meet you in Escalante.

"Oh, Shadow … you sweetheart!" she cooed, as she bent over to pet her. A little more calmly now, Agatha turned to me, "Well, I woke up this morning and Eugene was nowhere to be found. I looked outside and the pickup is still here. I checked over at the terrace, the bath house, and on the walking trail. Nope, no sign of him. It was only after I came back inside the trailer that I saw this," she grabbed at the note and shook it for effect.

"Who did he go with? Did you check in with Andrew or Leslie?" JJ was concerned.

"I have no idea! I'm telling you … *I don't know!*" She was agitated again.

"Let's call him … what's his cell phone number?" I pulled mine out of my back pocket.

"He don't use those things…" she harrumphed.

"Okay, well … We'll go find Andrew," Greg quickly inserted. "We'll see if we can determine who Eugene left with. Be right back." Greg and JJ set off across the park.

"Were you guys planning on going to Escalante next?" I asked.

"I don't know!" She sighed out of exasperation. "He makes all the plans and I rarely know what they are until we're actually going!"

Alexis and I exchanged a look. Then she offered, "Agatha, let's go grab some lemonade or something." My friend gently took Agatha's arm and led her toward their camper.

"Oh, I need something stronger than *lem-on-ade…*" she emphatically stated. "Got some vodka to put in that *lemonade?*"

I decided to track Greg and JJ down and headed toward the terrace, where I could see them talking to a few people. I left Alexis to deal with the upset woman. By the time I caught up to them, they had found Andrew, and I caught the tail end of their conversation.

"…it must have been really early," Andrew was saying.

Greg saw me approaching and said to me, "I've talked to several people and no one saw anything." He turned back to Andrew, "Are there cameras set up that monitor the entrance and exit?"

"Oh, yeah, sure. Let's go up to my trailer and take a look."

We followed Andrew into his forty-foot Solitude S-Class fifth-wheel. We stepped inside and I was instantly distracted by how beautiful their place was. The thing was enormous—and I thought Greg's RV was something; this was the most elegant house on wheels that I had ever seen. In tones of gray and white, there was beautiful laminate wood flooring, two full leather sofas, a recliner, and a huge living room TV just above a gas fireplace. The kitchen actually had a full-size refrigerator—not the travel size one Greg's had. And it had *an island* ... holy smokes! This was fancy. Apparently, the guys didn't notice my slobbering over the place; they had already settled at Andrew's desk. Yes, there was even a little alcove with an office setup: computer, monitor, desk, and chair. Amazing.

"We'll start reviewing footage after midnight. If I remember correctly, I saw them visiting with folks on the terrace until about that time." Andrew started the software on the computer and we watched the monitor over his shoulder.

"Ah, here ... about four in the morning. See." He pointed to a van that came through the entrance and turned right. "Let's pull up the camera from the other end of the property and see where he went."

The other camera was apparently set up just over the dog park. It faced north which captured our camps and the few around us.

"Yep. Look. There's Eugene," JJ said. "That van looks similar to one we took today, doesn't it, Greg?"

"Sure does." Greg agreed and then asked Andrew, "Is

there a way to zoom in? There may be a decal on the door."

"Let's see ..." he used his mouse to select the screenshot and then scrolled to zoom in. "That looks like something there," he pointed out.

"Back Canyon Outfitters," I read out loud. "That's the same company we just used today, isn't it? Look, the little kayak logo—that's the same!"

Andrew nodded his head slowly saying, "That's strange. We are good friends with the owner; why wouldn't he have mentioned to me there would be such an early pickup?"

"You didn't book this for Eugene, did you?" Greg asked Andrew.

"Nope. Those two haven't been receptive to us handling anything for them. They could have received the same discount your group got if they had."

"Why wouldn't Agatha know about this?" I pondered.

Greg stood. "Well, thank you, Andrew! Really appreciate your help. We'll go back and see what more Agatha can tell us." Andrew stood and they shook hands. "Really nice rig, by the way. Love how much room you have in here." Greg and Andrew talked RV living for a few more minutes and then we were off.

"I didn't see the driver in that footage, did you?" I asked.

Greg shook his head after contemplating.

"It seems he arranged something prior, otherwise, how would the outfitter company know where to come pick him up?"

"Maybe there are more notes or some type of clue in their trailer? Let's see if we can invite ourselves in?" Greg had a gleam in his eye; I think he wanted to solve a mystery.

CHAPTER NINE

When we returned, Shadow was snoozing on the ground, just below the two lying back in zero-gravity chairs, enjoying the shade. We grabbed beers from our cooler and chairs from our site. Immediately, we could tell that Agatha was much more relaxed than when we had left her earlier.

"You all look quite comfortable. Mind if we join this party?"

"Does anyone know where my husband went?" Agatha slurred slightly.

"Libby, there's more 'Rum-n-ades' in the pitcher in the fridge if you'd like," Alexis offered.

"Rum ... a- what?"

"Well, we didn't have vodka. Agatha mixed up some lemonade and rum ... we're calling it Rum-n-ade! Never mixed the two before—but it's *delicious*," she emphasized. "So refreshing!"

"How much have you had already?"

They both giggled, which told me they'd had a few.

"I'll stick with the beer I've opened, but maybe another time. It does sounds refreshing."

"Does anyone know where my husband went?!" Agatha shouted.

Greg patiently told her what we discovered on the camera's footage. "It seems like he booked an adventure with Back Canyon Outfitters. Does that ring a bell? Did he talk about that?"

"I don't know! He talks all the time. How am I supposed to keep up?"

"Agatha, would you mind if we helped you look for another note? Or, some receipt. Something that might explain why he left without you. We know from the other note, he's headed for Escalante. But, *when* are you supposed to meet him?"

"We have reservations here for another night. We're supposed to leave *tomorrow!*" she shouted. "I guess I'm supposed to meet him *tomorrow.*"

She didn't address us helping her search the trailer so Greg dropped that for now.

Alexis held up her hand like a school kid asking permission to speak next. "Agatha, do you drive the RV?"

"Oh yeah. I drive it all the time. No problem." Her hand waved Alexis' question off and she took another sip of lemonade.

"And, since he left with someone else, how are you going to drive both the RV and the truck with a boat in tow?" JJ asked.

Agatha's eyes flew open. "Well, I don't know!" she

yelled out. Her face scrunched up and her hands swept around. "I suppose I just hook 'em all up together. *We'll figure it out!*"

JJ and Greg shared a perplexed glance at one another. Then, JJ calmly asked, "Did he leave you the keys?"

"Oh, for heaven's sake! I don't know!" Flustered, and seemingly angry, she struggled to get standing and began to head over to their site.

We all got up and followed Agatha. The RV keys were still in the lock on the outside of the door. She pulled them out proudly, "Here they are!"

We all chuckled with nervousness. *How do these two manage on their trips together?*

"Are the truck's keys on that same ring?" JJ asked.

She started flipping through the metal … there was a huge collection of keys on one ring. Finally, she realized something. "Uh, no. Nope, the truck doesn't have a key," she stated emphatically.

"Ah, so it's a key fob then, right?" JJ's eyes kept contact with hers, all the while practicing the patience of Job. She seemed paralyzed for a few seconds.

"Umm, it's one of those … *you know*, it's black and silver about this size," she said agitated, but her fingers demonstrating something a couple inches in size.

"Yes, it's a fob. I assume it's inside? Let's look for it." Greg opened the door and encouraged her to step up, assisting as she was still a bit tipsy.

We traipsed in behind her, letting our eyes adjust to darkness. Agatha immediately headed to the console between the driver and passenger seats. She started rummaging through papers, maps, and personal effects. No key fob.

Greg focused on the dining table. There, too, were papers, more maps, a couple metal boxes, and food wrappers.

Alexis and I made our way to the rear of their camper toward the bedroom. Perhaps it was left in a pair of jeans or a shirt pocket.

After everyone filed their way through surface clutter, and examined every pocket on the tossed-aside clothing, we came to the conclusion that the truck key was not here.

I whispered to Greg, "Think we should check to make sure it wasn't left in the truck?" He agreed that was a good idea and snuck out quietly to check.

Agatha had long since given up and sat on her sofa looking defeated. "I don't understand why he'd leave without me." My heart ached for this woman. I think I'd be in a state of panic, too.

Greg came back inside, looked at me shaking his head. No keys. Truck was locked.

"Should we call the police? Are we concerned Eugene may be in danger?" Alexis asked the group.

JJ was quick to respond. "He hasn't even been gone twenty-four hours. The police won't consider him a missing person. And, he left a note indicating where he was going—so he's not technically 'missing'—we know where he went, right?"

"Good point," I said. "Well, they're paid up for one more night at this campground. Eugene indicated to 'meet in Escalante' so we're all assuming that means tomorrow. Agatha, are you concerned about Eugene's safety?"

"Oh, no … that man does what he wants, when he wants. He's tough. No, I'm just upset he left me here." She scoffed, "What does he mean, 'meet in Escalante'?

He's leaving all the packing to *me*! I don't want to stay here tonight all by myself!" I thought she was going to start crying.

"Agatha, you said you're okay driving the RV, right?" I asked. "We can leave the truck and boat here until we find Eugene."

Greg, who was standing behind Agatha and outside of her view, signaled the *too much drinky-drinky* motion with his hands. Crap, I'd already forgotten how much she'd had to drink.

"Of course, I can drive this thing!" Agatha continued to look put out. "I never have, but I … I can get along just fine on my own!"

We all stared in disbelief. She had just told us earlier that she drives it all the time. Now, she says she never has.

"Uh. Ok, well, we can help you," I started looking around at my friends encouragingly as they continued the staring contest with me. "Yes, yes, we can help you load up and get to Escalante. We'll find Eugene and then, tomorrow morning, we'll be on our way to Bryce Canyon. Just as planned."

After an uncomfortable exchange of looks between my friends, Alexis spoke up. "It is only a thirty-minute drive to Escalante. Sure, we … we can do this!" Her radiant smile warmed my heart. JJ and Greg were still trying to sort out exactly why the plan was changing. None of this was what we had planned to do on vacation, but then again, doesn't that make for some of the best adventures?

CHAPTER TEN

We decided Greg was the best one to drive the RV. I rode with him and Agatha. Alexis and JJ followed in our rental vehicle and we were off to Escalante.

Agatha's spirit had lifted considerably and I sat talking to her at the dining table, after I had made space amongst the metal boxes and the paperwork that were placed now on the bench seat. Shadow made her way under the table and rested comfortably on my feet.

"What are these boxes for? Ammunition?"

"I think originally, yes, they were for ammunition. Eugene's treasures go in there."

"What type of treasures?"

"Oh, he's always searching for the next big *find*. Always!" She was getting animated again.

"Is that what you do on your travels then?" Greg asked

from the driver's seat.

"When I met Eugene, he had just lost his beloved wife of twenty some odd years." She pulled out her toothpick and started picking as she talked. I ignored the grossness. "The two of them were always treasure hunting. As he tells the story, that's what attracted him to her in the first place. She came from a long line of adventurers who happened to also be very wealthy."

"What kind of adventures? This sounds fascinating…" I knew there was more to this couple and I wanted to hear it all.

"There was something about her parents' passing—they left a trove of valuables, specifically asking for them to be carefully watched after and cared for."

"They?"

"Oh, Evelyn and her brother, Walter." She kept picking at the teeth. "Now, you see … Walter was much younger than Evelyn so they weren't all that close. Lived in different cities. I guess there was a big hoopla between them when she learned that Walter had sneakily started burying these relics all over the US!" Her eyes bulged as she continued, "Yes! I'm serious … he took them right out of the security deposit boxes from the bank and hid them in varying places!"

"Wow…" I was mesmerized by her story.

"Well, she and Eugene were bound and determined to find each and every relic, come hell or high water! So, they set out on this many-years-long journey. Of course, then, he made a deathbed promise to her that he'd never give up. Now look at him … ninety-five years old and *he's still at it*. He won't stop until he dies."

Greg had been listening intently as he drove. "What

happened to Evelyn, if you don't mind my asking?"

"Cancer. She had a rough time with it—two and half years fighting through."

"Oh, I'm so sorry to hear that." I couldn't imagine what it was like for Eugene, but also, this poor woman retelling the story and clearly aware that Evelyn was the love of his life. How was *she* coping? I supposed enough time had passed now that it was just part of their tale.

Greg broke the uncomfortable silence. "What type of *relics* are these anyway?"

"Oh, I don't even know specifically. He's secretive to this day about that. I just go along on the expedition to keep him happy." Her gaze turned wistful. "He just loves all this, you know." I got the distinct feeling she did not, but it was clear she loved him and would do anything to please him.

I was curious. "Did they ever figure out what the brother's motivation was ... hiding these objects?"

She laughed. "I'm not sure they could have ever figured out that guy. As I understand, he was always the dreamer and some say he was a con-artist. I don't know about that. He was also a philanthropist and accomplished a lot in his day, helping the needy, so I can't imagine him conning people, but that was the rumor. He lived minimally and was always eager to share his great fortune. The problem was—these items were also part of Evelyn's fortune, too."

"Was? He's no longer living either?" I asked.

"Nope, died about five years ago."

"And have *any* of the valuables ever been found?" Greg asked.

"Not that I'm aware of." She set her pick on the table and took a drink of water.

"Fascinating." I picked up my phone and texted Alexis, asking her to remind me to tell her more about this later. *She's not going to believe what we've learned.*

Within half an hour, we were at the outskirts of Escalante. The meager town probably had no more than a thousand people living there, but travelers frequented it because of all the nearby national and state parks. Surrounded by the sandstone canyons and cliffs, washes, as well as the Dixie National Forest in the distance, there was much to set out and do from Escalante.

"Which RV park are we headed to?" Greg shouted from the front seat as we approached town.

Agatha sat staring. I waited for a few seconds and then wondered if she had heard the question.

"Agatha? We're here in Escalante. Where's the RV park?"

"How should I know?!" she retorted.

I headed up to the front passenger seat before she could detect my frustration with her. I started shuffling through all the papers that were still scattered on the floor. Surely, they had a reservation slip or something. It was apparent these two printed *everything* out.

"Hon, why don't you pull into that gas station over there to your right? We'll figure it out," I quietly suggested.

We got stopped safely off to the side of a huge parking lot at Sinclair's. JJ and Alexis pulled in behind us. I continued looking fervently for anything that might give us a clue where we should go. The rest of the group were already stretching their legs outside and they took Shadow for her restroom break.

I remembered that there were more stacks of paper at the seat I'd just come from so I headed back to the dining table. Curiosity overcame me and I opened one of the metal boxes. Inside, I found an old pocket knife, a few ancient coins, and several pieces of folded paper. I took out the first square and started to unfold it. The writing was barely legible, but I think it said, "Southwest." I grabbed the next one and opened it. Same handwriting—*Salton Sea*. And then, the last note in the similar shaky script said—*Big Fish*. It also had a symbol drawing of a fish. *Are these some of the treasures they've found?* I wondered. *If so, I think these two are on a wild-goose chase.* I opened the second metal container. There were more maps in that one. Sheesh, how many maps could one own? I closed the boxes and continued to rummage through the paperwork sitting on the seat, when I noticed something. I got up, moved the seat cushion away, and there it was ... the truck's key fob!

I slipped out of the RV and joined up with the others on their short walk in the field at the back of the gas station. Greg broke off from the others and asked if I'd found anything; I let him know there was nothing useful.

"So now what?" he asked.

"I'm starting to think this was a bad idea—offering to get involved. Oh! But, guess what? I found the truck key!"

"Oh, good! That will help. Where was it?"

"Stuck in the dining room seat cushions."

"Too bad we didn't figure that out earlier before driving the gas guzzler out here. Oh well. Hopefully, we'll find Eugene and they'll stay the night here. We could always bring their truck and boat out to them tomorrow, maybe." He saw the look on my face. That's not at all what I want to get involved doing. "And, I know what you mean about getting involved. But, really, we had to—we couldn't leave her on her own."

"I know. And, of course, I want to be helpful. I think I just find myself frustrated with her inconsistencies and she's not really *helping*, is she? Or, is it just me?" I was beginning to feel bad that I kept letting her fluster me.

"It's got to be difficult at their age. We're here and we can be helpful—that's who we are."

"*I know*, right?" I exclaimed. "I sure wouldn't want to be in her shoes right now. And, I think I'd be thankful for the 'younguns' swooping in to help!" I giggled.

Alexis came over to us as JJ and Agatha decided to venture into the convenience store for a snack. "So, what's the plan now?"

Greg and I filled her in on everything Agatha shared on our drive, and also what she didn't share.

She just shook her head, "Unbelievable. But, it looked like there were only a few RV parks as we pulled into town. Maybe we just hop in the Jeep and go scope it all out. Leave the RV here—It'd be easier that way."

I agreed. "Certainly, the hosts would be able to tell us if the Walkers had a reservation. We may even find Eugene kicking back with them, enjoying himself a happy hour drink by now," I chuckled.

We walked back to the RV and once Agatha and JJ had made their way back to us, we loaded up into the Jeep. Agatha snugly fit in between Alexis and me in the backseat with Shadow at our feet and off we went in search of Eugene.

CHAPTER ELEVEN

It was getting dark out now and we had exhausted all our RV park resources. No reservations in the name of Walker and no one had seen a man of Eugene's description either. Despair was beginning to set in. I, for one, had hoped to be back at our dark skies' campground having a nice steak dinner and settling in for the night already. Instead, we were standing in a gas station parking lot again and submitting a stolen vehicle report with the police.

The RV was nowhere to be found.

"I suppose this wasn't the best idea we've had..." Alexis pointed out.

"He's dead! I just know he's dead!" Agatha was crying on JJ's shoulder.

"No, Agatha. You can't think that way. We'll find him."

"*Why?*" she cried. "Why did he leave me?"

None of us knew the answer to that question, but we certainly wanted to find out. And, who stole their RV?

After the police left, Greg suggested that we should head back to Kanab in the Jeep. There was nothing more we could do here tonight. So, we loaded up and headed back down Hwy 89 to Kanab. Agatha was beside herself. Despite the tough exterior, she was scared, sad, and feeling hopeless now.

We set Agatha up on the sofa sleeper in our RV, agreeing that we'd all caravan back to Escalante in the morning if Eugene didn't show up before then. As unpredictable as they were, I could just picture waking up in the morning with their truck and boat missing—Agatha out searching for her beloved. For now, Shadow cuddled with her, so that provided some comfort.

In the morning, Agatha was still with us and I quickly looked out the window. Nope, no Eugene. No RV across the way. That would have been too easy. Instead, I got up and started making coffee. Agatha was sitting at the dining table just staring out the window.

"Good morning!" I said as cheerfully as I could on just a few hours' sleep.

She nodded, but never made eye contact—she just kept staring out the window. Then, quietly, she asked, "Do you remember that outfitter's place at the edge of town?"

My brain had to catch up. I assumed she meant in Escalante so I attempted to recall—there were the RV parks, gas station, a country store. Were there other businesses?

"No, don't remember that. What was the name?" I asked.

"Not sure. I think the sign showed a boat ... or something."

"Why are you asking?"

"I think he had a guide take him on an excursion."

"Yes, remember that JJ and Greg told us that a guide picked him up early yesterday morning. But, did you remember something about him scheduling it?"

"Not sure."

Ugh. The vagueness ... the inconsistencies. I was about to pull my hair out. Coffee first.

Greg walked in and gave me a warm kiss. "Good morning, Agatha," he said to her. He got the same warm reception that I did. I met his knowing look. Poor woman. She's distraught.

"Hey, sweetie. Agatha was asking about an outfitter just on the outskirts of town—in Escalante. Do you remember seeing one yesterday?"

"Yeah, I remember thinking their sign looked very similar to the company we used for the slot canyon experience. I wonder if they operate out of both locations?"

"It's possible. Bet Siri would know. Or, if you talk to Andrew ... he'd know. The place was owned by his friend, remember?"

"We'll look into it. And, since we're headed back there today, we could always go by and scope it out ourselves."

She perked up, looking over at us with a slight smile. "They probably know where he is."

"Agatha, I never asked, but is this normal for Eugene to just run off without you?"

"Nah. But, he does a lot of things without thinking, so it's not surprising. Just irritating." She accepted the cup of coffee I handed to her. "Got any cream?"

"Yep." I opened the refrigerator and pulled it out.

"Sugar too?" I asked as I handed the cream over.

"No."

Maybe just once she could give a 'please' or a 'thank you,' I thought that generation was better at the niceties.

Greg laced up his shoes and grabbed keys. "I'll be right back. Need to review a few things with JJ before we start packing up."

Agatha and I sat in silence, enjoying our coffee. I pulled out my iPhone while she continued to stare across the way, willing Eugene to return quickly and on his own. I looked up local news for the fun of it. It was news out of Salt Lake City so I doubted I'd see anything related to a stolen RV or a missing man, but it couldn't hurt to look. I was surprised to read several headlines that were regional—out of St. George, Panguitch, and a few tidbits from Kanab too. I wouldn't have expected that. These towns were so small.

The video I watched was of a man who had just caught the largest trout the state had ever seen from Panguitch Lake. He held it up and the smile was infectious. I just loved to see someone enjoying their life's passion and that was certainly the case with this young man. Agatha must have seen my smile.

"Whatcha smiling at?" she asked.

I played the video again for her to see. "Where's that?" she wondered.

"It says … Pang-u-itch. Up the road from here."

"Eugene loves fishing. He'd like it there," she softly spoke, drifting her attention back to the window.

Greg and JJ came in, and JJ squeezed in beside Agatha. "How are you doing today, Agatha?" The tall blonde man put his arms around her for a hug. "I hope you slept well."

She smiled big for the handsome JJ. I think she enjoyed

the attention.

"I slept decent. You know, for a strange place … decent."

"Do you all want breakfast burritos?" I asked. "I'm willing to make them, if you'll eat them."

All of their eyes indicated yes, but Greg brought us back to reality. "Hon, as great as that sounds right now, I think we should start making a move. We've got a lot to pack up and then we need to get on the road and go find Agatha's missing RV and husband."

"Yeah, unfortunately," JJ reluctantly agreed. "Alexis and I already had cereal and she's cleaning up and securing the kitchen now to go."

"Okay, we'll do those tomorrow then. We'll grab some fruit and power bars and get out of here."

"Hey! How am I supposed to move *that*?" Agatha pointed out the window to the truck.

I completely forgot that I had stashed her truck fob in my pocket yesterday in Escalante. "Oh! Agatha, I found it! Wait…" I went to the bedroom to dig into the hiking pants I'd worn the day before. Running back out, I handed them to her. "I'm sorry, I meant to give these to you yesterday. They were in the cushions—at your dining table where we had been sitting."

Her whole demeanor changed and she looked like a child on Christmas Day. "Oh, thank the heavens above. I thought for sure he left them at home. I've always said we should carry both sets—but he always says to leave one set at home. Well, now, how's that going to help us on the road? We should each have our own set!" And, she was right. Not helpful at all.

* * *

It only took about an hour for our three camps to clean up, load, and secure everything, before we were ready to leave. I agreed to ride with Agatha in her truck. Greg would lead the caravan, with JJ and Alexis picking up the tail-end and keeping an eye on Agatha's tow load.

"This truck is fancy! Look at all those buttons," I said after sitting in the plush leather seat and buckling up.

"I don't even know what half of these are for!" she lamented.

"I imagine. Looks complicated." It was hard to imagine how older people figured this stuff out—everything these days is electronic and run by computer. Like the ignition, it was a button—no need for a key, as we discovered. But, holy smokes, there was a button for *everything*.

She did well driving the large truck with the boat trailer. I was concerned she might not even be able to see over the steering wheel, but the seat adjusted quite high and it all worked out. I noticed that Greg was setting a manageable pace considering we were towing and I was appreciative of that. She maintained a safe distance from Greg without going impossibly slow.

"I just wish he'd get off this treasure hunting kick. It's not even his family's belongings," she started.

"Yeah, both the ex-wife and her brother have now passed. It is curious why he'd continue the search."

"I'd just like to stay home for a while. All this traveling is wearing me out."

"Where is home?"

"Colorado. Near Colorado Springs."

"Oh, okay, so not too far away. At least in this same region. What brought you guys here to Utah … was there some clue or something the brother said before he died that indicated he buried the stuff here?"

"Honestly, I'm not sure. We have been everywhere—from Oregon to Vermont and Florida to Arizona. Holy crap, we haven't stopped in *years*."

I was exhausted just hearing that. Even though I love traveling, and I certainly would be lured by the excitement of a treasure hunt, I could never imagine doing that for *years*. And, unsuccessfully at that. Nope. Couldn't pay me enough. *Wait, is that what's keeping him going? Has someone offered to pay him big bucks if he finds these items?*

"Agatha, do you know whether Walter had family? Or, maybe, did Evelyn have aunts or uncles that also knew about this treasure?"

She thought about it for a moment. "I think Walter had a son ... or, was it a daughter? I can't remember. Eugene disregarded that side of her family when they started this funny business of hiding stuff. Oh, and they kept coming around with their hands out, too. Why should he give them anything?"

"Okay, but there were descendants, right? Do you think Eugene made contact with them?"

"I don't think so. He's never mentioned anything."

It seemed possible to me that the extended family might have been involved. But, were they directly involved in his disappearance yesterday? I didn't think that was as likely. Perhaps JJ would be open to a little research, being that he's a detective. I would love to know where this grandson and his family reside now.

"Agatha, when I was looking for the key fob, I accidentally tipped over one of those metal boxes." *Okay, maybe that was just a little white lie.* "Some coins, a pocket knife, and some folded papers fell out. They appeared to be very old. Are they some of the items that Eugene has found on your expeditions?"

"We found those at Lake Powell! What a find indeed!" She certainly got excited. "He said he'd get the knife and coins appraised—he thinks they date back into the 1800s."

Suddenly, I remembered that JJ and I had found an empty container on the cove shore the evening we went boating. And, on our way out, we saw Agatha and Eugene's boat pulling in. But, the box we saw—although metal—did not look like the ones in their RV.

"At Lake Powell, you found them … was that the night we passed by you leaving that cove?"

She looked deep in thought and I worried she'd take her attention away from the road. Then, she laughed, "You have a great memory, dear. Yes! I remember now. We were headed there to continue his search. He was sure there was more stuff to find, just certain of it."

"How did he know where at Lake Powell to look for these items?"

"He receives clues."

"From who?"

She stared at me. I indicated by pointing that she should watch the road. "Now, how would I know that?" The snarky reaction made me wonder if she was playing me or if she really was *that* clueless about what her husband was up to.

"So, he's never indicated to you *how* he knows to go to certain locations and *where* to look?"

"I told you—he has clues!"

Okay, I was obviously not asking the right questions. It was time to sit back and enjoy the ride; I was getting nowhere. I just prayed that we found him soon—I wanted answers from Eugene. Was the folded note we found another clue? Had Eugene dropped it? I found myself getting excited at the possibilities. Then, I stopped myself—I just needed to get back to vacationing with my friends. *Why do I always insert myself into things that are not my business?* But, then, on the other hand, wasn't it concerning when an older gentleman went missing and his wife obviously needed help? They *need* us. No, I couldn't turn my back on them now. *We need to help them find their way back to each other, and I need to make sure Eugene gets the clue he left behind at Powell.*

We arrived in Escalante near noon. The campground that Greg had arranged was on our left as we entered town. Our caravan pulled up to the sign that indicated 'Registration' and Greg got out to check in the group. Shadow was getting restless, as well as curious, about where we'd landed now.

Once we were all settled in our reserved spots, I got Shadow on the leash and took her over to the campground's dog park where she could be off-leash to run. I threw the ball from one end of the run to the other until she had worn off her puppy energy. On the way back to the RVs, we disrupted the peace at several sites as we encircled the park. The other tenants' dogs didn't like us walking by, but Shadow just woofed 'hi' to them as we passed. Or, at least that's what I had made up in my mind. Who knows, maybe she was taunting them and trying to rile them up?

Just before we turned the corner onto our row, Shadow's attention suddenly shifted the other direction. I spun around, trying to keep my balance and hold of the leash. "What..." I saw immediately what it was that captured her attention. Eugene had just walked into the office! We followed.

I didn't even consider that dogs may not be allowed in the office—we just walked in anyway. He was at the registration desk; no one else other than the clerk was in the room.

"Eugene?!" I walked over and tapped him on the shoulder.

He turned; confusion was etched in his brows.

"It's Libby…"

He looked down at Shadow. "Oh, hi! What are you doing here? Are you following me?" he teased, winking at me.

I stood there, staring in disbelief for more than a moment. He looked good—certainly not kidnapped or out of food or water. His casual demeanor intimated that he had no concern that anyone would be looking for him. He handed his credit card to the clerk, who went about the business of assigning a site to Eugene.

"Agatha's been looking for you—she's been sick with worry!" Then, I turned to the clerk myself. "We've already paid for their site. We just got here ten minutes ago or so— three sites, Greg Lawson the reservation would be under, but I do not remember our site numbers." The nice lady went about looking that up. Meanwhile, Eugene looked confused about why I was inserting myself in his check-in process.

He seemed indifferent about Agatha being upset. "I told her I'd meet her here."

"How did you get here?"

He pointed just outside the door we had just entered by. Outside sat their RV, pulled up alongside the curb. *What the hell?*

The clerk verified the reservations and I walked out with Eugene; we got in his rig and I pointed the direction to where the truck and boat were parked. Thankfully, there was enough overflow parking at this campground when we had to move them from the space that we'd now park the RV in.

The looks on Greg, Agatha, JJ, and Alexis' faces as the RV pulled up were priceless. Mouths agape, eyebrows furrowed, then their lips began making an O shape and hands reaching up to cover their surprise. Eugene maneuvered the gearshift into Park and set the emergency brake, but didn't turn off the engine. We both got out and Shadow jumped down.

As fast as Agatha's little legs could propel her, she ran to Eugene's side. Tears were already flowing down her face. She pulled him into a hug and I was concerned they both were going to go down; they seemed unbalanced. Then, she slugged him in the arm—hard. "Where the hell did you go?!" Another punch. "Why did you *leave me*?"

He maintained his balance as he backed up a couple steps. "Whoa! Stop hitting me, Agatha." He rubbed his arm, scowling. "I told you I'd meet you here. Didn't you get my note?" His head turned, looking at the nearby campers who'd started to gather amongst the commotion.

Greg understood Agatha's anger as she walked away. He waved off the bystanders, telling them everything was okay. Then, he stepped up to shake Eugene's hand. "Good to see you again. You had us worried, Eugene."

JJ took his turn greeting the elderly gentleman. "I see you found the RV," he nodded his head toward their camper.

"Yes. Yes. It was nice of you to leave it for me over there

at that gas station. At least, I assumed you had something to do with it—Agatha couldn't manage…"

I had enough. "Eugene. You can't just run off on a whim without telling your wife! You left her with an RV, a truck, and a boat. How did you expect her to 'meet' you anywhere?"

He gave me a blank look.

I continued to ramble. "Then, after we came here looking for you, left the RV at the gas station *temporarily*— we thought the RV was stolen! If you thought we had left it, why didn't you wait with the camper for us to get back last night? You drove off with it and we filed a police report!"

For a second, it appeared he just checked out. Logic, reasoning, whatever you want to call it, just wasn't getting through. Or, he didn't care.

Greg took over and calmly stated, "Eugene, we all became worried—both for you and for Agatha. We saw you leave with someone in a van early yesterday morning. Who was that?"

"Oh! That nice man. He really needs to wash his hair, but he was lovely."

"He was with an outdoorsman outfitter group, correct?" I asked.

"Oh yeah. Yep. They arrange expeditions all the time."

I decided to try a different tactic with Eugene since I hadn't gotten anywhere with my questioning. Instead, I smiled now, my voice took on a high-pitched excited tone, hoping I could keep him talking. "Wow! That sounds fun. What expedition did you go on?"

It worked. His eyes shone bright; his recently whitened teeth were on full display through his huge smile. "I wanted to see one of the slot canyons. There's one not far from here," he said, pointing north from where we were standing. "But, that's not where he took me."

JJ tried. "So, where did he take you?"

Agatha started waving her hands wildly in the air and moved to break up the group. "This is pointless. He sneaks around all the time and he's not gonna tell us squat." She grabbed his arm and pulled him over to the RV. After a few more colorful words between them, she pulled keys out of her pocket and stomped over to move the truck and boat to the overflow parking area. Once she pulled out, Eugene maneuvered the RV into the campsite with the help of JJ and Greg to get it just so.

Alexis and I just stood to the side, watching the whole spectacle. I got the idea that was exactly what other campers were doing also. That was confirmed when I glanced to my right and saw blinds quickly move back into place as the couple next door to us saw me look over at them. Agatha was not a happy camper when she arrived back. She stormed into the RV and we didn't see her the rest of the afternoon.

* * *

The afternoon was warm and pleasant. We all got settled in and enjoyed some time kicking our feet up, hoping that we'd learn more about where Eugene had been all day yesterday.

"I'm glad we didn't set out for Bryce Canyon this afternoon. All this drama has been exhausting," I commented.

Greg put down the map he was examining. "Yeah, it's interesting that we came on vacation to get away from drama and then we meet those two." He casually glanced over to Eugene's site across the way from us.

"Think they'll still be here by morning?" Alexis mumbled, face down on her chaise lounge.

JJ answered, "That's the magical question, isn't it?"

"Agatha was telling us yesterday," I pointed between Greg and me, "and then a little more on the way over here today that most of their travels revolve around searching for treasure that belonged to his former wife," I added.

"What?!" Alexis sat up and crossed her long legs under her, leaning toward me. "What *treasure*?"

Looking to Greg to corroborate what I was saying, I continued. "Seems as though his first wife, Evelyn, as she told us was her name, came from money. Something about her long since deceased family members leaving them centuries-old relics. Then her brother got his hands on them and has squandered a bunch of it." I took a long sip of my iced tea. "Actually, that's not the most accurate way of describing. It seems as though he's spent years hiding coins, and old stuff in general, all over the U.S. Eugene follows clues, but she had no idea how he obtains said clues. I don't know ... the more we're around them, the crazier it all sounds. Are they just making this stuff up?"

Greg had been listening intently, and nodding his head. "And, I nearly forgot, but I finally did get Eugene to open up a *little bit*," he indicated with his fingers how little. "While Agatha went away earlier and we were parking the RV, he was lamenting about how nosy she is and 'his former in-laws are just none of her business'. Do you think that's who he went off with overnight?"

"She seems to think that he hasn't had contact with them in years. Ever since Evelyn's brother, Walter, kept asking them for money. That's what she told me this morning."

"If they were a wealthy family, why would this brother be asking Eugene for money?"

I just shrugged. *How do we know any of this is true?*

Alexis asked, "Where's Evelyn now? Did they divorce, or…?"

"Oh. No. Unfortunately, she passed away about twenty years ago. Cancer."

"And her brother is still alive?" JJ asked.

"No, he passed about five years ago."

"So, that answers that question … can't be either of them he ran off with yesterday." Greg set aside the map, and looked over at me. "Why don't we venture down to that outfitter's place and ask some questions?"

I perked up. Even though there was one part of me that was exhausted of the older couple's drama, I was extremely curious. "Ok. Wanna go, guys?" I turned to Alexis and JJ.

"Nah, man. I'm enjoying relaxing time." JJ took a drink from his beer bottle. Alexis just groaned and rolled back over, presumably to take a nap.

Greg and I got up, went to our RV, leashed Shadow, and gathered our belongings to set out in the Jeep. It had been several days since Greg and I had wandered off on our own. I found myself really excited to spend time just the two of us. And Shadow, of course.

We turned right out of the RV park and ventured down the main drag for a couple blocks. On our right, there it was: Back Canyon Outfitters. We pulled in and parked next to a Land Rover.

"I guess you can rent equipment here, too." I pointed out the Land Rover occupants to Greg. They were loading up a few kayaks on their racks. "That would be fun, to go kayaking!"

Shadow seemed to agree with a little extra bounce in her step. Greg nodded as he held the door open for us. Shadow let out a woof as soon as we entered. We recognized one of our guides from the slot canyon adventure. He had been the quiet one so we hadn't gotten to know him as well as our other guide, but nonetheless, it was definitely the same one.

Greg held out his hand and the man with 'Bramm' noted on his nametag approached him. "Hey, man, good to see you again ... Marley, wasn't it?" Greg said. The dreadlocked man's face didn't indicate any recognition. "We did the slot canyon hike a couple days ago. Along with our two friends ... and," he looked down at Shadow, trailing off when he realized that effort was fruitless. "Anyway, we're here to rent a couple of kayaks. Where do you row around here by the way?"

Greg noticed the look of surprise on my face. I didn't know that's what we were here for, but now it appeared that my comment earlier had sparked his interest too. Or, it was a ruse. I went along regardless.

The guy, still staring at the floor without eye-to-eye contact, turned to go behind the counter. Shadow's ears were back and she moved slowly next to me as we all followed the man to the front counter, even though we hadn't been invited to follow. He grabbed a brochure, leaned over the glass countertop, and quietly stated, "Most people do the Escalante River." He pointed to a map, "Here is the trailhead where you put in ... take out is at Lake Powell. Well, normally it is. The drought has made it slightly complicated, so right now, it's a hike out at Coyote

Gulch. Mile 72."

"Wow, that's long!" I stated.

"You experienced?" The guide never looked directly at us; he kept staring at the map. "This isn't exactly an easy float."

"We both can typically handle Class II-III rapids. We're not expert or extreme kayakers. How tough is it?"

"It has its level of difficulties along the way, but no more than Class III. You should be fine." He turned and grabbed another piece of paper. "Here are our kayak and rafting prices. We recommend having a guide, but we rent to individuals as well. When you book as a group, we'll haul your equipment. We have a van—picks up and drops off from any location here in Escalante. Where you stayin'?" he asked.

"Over at Escalante RV Resort," Greg answered.

Our older hipster guide's phone chimed, he looked down at it and swiped at the screen. His eyes finally made contact with us. He expressed confusion, then quickly looked down again, gathered the papers and busied himself. Greg and I looked at each other questioningly. Shadow let out a low growl.

"Shadow. Shh." I reprimanded and pulled the leash a bit tighter.

"So, if we want to book a group outing for tomorrow, what's available?" I asked.

Still facing away from me, the man mumbled, "No availability tomorrow."

Greg was getting impatient. Shadow was getting restless, and she watched this guy very cautiously. I wanted to know more about why he was acting so weird. He hadn't recognized us from the previous excursion, he had barely looked at us now, and all of a sudden, he wasn't being helpful when he could have told us from the start that no rentals were available.

"Have we done something to upset you?" Greg asked calmly.

"Nah. Just no availability."

"Why wouldn't you have just told us that to begin with?" I inquired.

Shadow growled a low rumble again, but remained seated.

"Listen man, forget the rentals," Greg moved closer in front of the man, trying to get him to look up again. "Did you pick up an elderly man in Kanab really early yesterday morning?"

Shadow understood; her anxiety level piqued. She stood, let out a bark.

The man glared at Shadow, then turned away again. Greg was sick of his rudeness. He reached out and grabbed his arm to turn him around. "What's the problem? Why can't you look at us and just answer our questions?"

"I don't know what you're talking about. I'm busy. We don't have availability so please go."

I took Greg's hand and squeezed it, nudging him to leave before this escalated further. Shadow lunged toward the guy as he walked away and I barely hung on to her leash. "What's gotten into you, Shadow? C'mon…" I looked to Greg. "We need to go. Forget this."

We walked out of the building and loaded into the Jeep. Sitting there staring at the front of the building, Greg just shook his head. "Something is very wrong in there and I cannot figure out what, or why."

"Extremely poor customer service?" I suggested.

"But, it's more than that. I am positive he was the one, or he knows, who picked up Eugene yesterday. If everything was on the up and up, why are both he and Eugene being so cagey?"

"Maybe it's none of our business? But then again, the guy here is in the tourist business. His customer service skills suck!"

Greg laughed. "I guess it isn't any concern of ours. Let's just go have fun with our friends. We need to figure out…" his voice trailed off as we watched the lanky long-haired man emerge from the front door, and quickly get into an old faded green truck with a trailered side-by-side in tow. He peeled off. "What's for dinner. Was that …?"

I nodded. "Yep, he just took off."

"Wanna follow?"

My heart raced and my eyes got huge. "Yes, I really do!" I smiled like a kid getting ready to play hide and seek.

CHAPTER TWELVE

Greg laughed as he backed out of the parking spot and quickly proceeded to the main street in town. We could see the truck and trailer about a quarter mile ahead and we followed it right out of town. Soon, we discovered we were headed in the direction of the small town of Boulder. Not knowing if he'd turn off before the town, we decided to pass a couple cars in front of us, but still maintain a car or two in between so we weren't noticed. When we got closer to Lower Calf Creek Falls, the truck signaled he was turning left. We continued ahead since it would be too obvious if we also turned down the road just behind him. Instead, we went about a mile up the road, found a safe place to turn around, and then we went back to the trailhead turnoff.

Turning right onto the Calf Creek Road, we kept our

eyes open for the green truck. We came upon a campground and decided to pull in. Driving around the loop, there was no sign of him so we proceeded to leave the campground and continued following signs to the trailhead. There was the green truck, along with half a dozen other SUVs in the parking lot. The side-by-side had been unloaded from the trailer and was nowhere in sight.

"Good thing we got some decent shoes on and have extra water bottles with us. Looks like we're going to take a little hike." Greg shut off the engine and we piled out. Shadow was excited to sniff this new area.

"How unexpected and fun!" I exclaimed. I was getting tired of riding in the car, even though we'd only ventured about sixteen miles. "I'm glad I called Lexi and they were fine just hanging. This looks like we'll be a while. At least, I'd like to make it a long hike, whether we find this guy again or not, do you?"

"Yeah. It's a beautiful day. Let's get exercise … and we'll see where this guy is going. He's probably just meeting a group—he is a guide after all."

Shadow ran as far as my arm would extend to the right of me, and then quickly shifted to the far left, pulling the leash and nearly twisting me around. "Hey, settle, girl…" I instructed. Greg leaned over and offered to take the leash so I let him. We walked over to the trail map.

"You could be right. What's with us thinking everyone is up to no good?" I laughed.

"Well, recently, no one *has* been up to any good!" I thought back on our past six months since we met. We were led on a wild-goose chase trying to find my client's daughter. Between camp hosts, a sketchy sheep herder, and the client's boyfriend, I didn't know who to trust. Then, not long after that, getting tangled up with drug lords wasn't any fun. Sheesh! It had been a crazy several months. And to think—Greg was still here with me, dealing with all my shenanigans. I smiled at the thought.

"Another hike should do us good though. Do you feel guilty we didn't wait till Alexis and JJ could do this with us?"

"No. I think it's good for us all to do separate things as well. We don't have to be glued to each other's hips." I smiled thinking of how much fun we'd already had. Then the smile left and I felt sudden confusion. I stopped. "Hey, isn't that Eugene's truck? Look, he has that same fishing bumper sticker..."

"Sure looks like it." Greg wandered over and peeked inside, then moved along the front touching the hood. "Still warm. Probably didn't arrive much before we did."

"Well, that's quite the coincidence, don't you think? I thought he was still back at the camp!"

He just shrugged. Shadow insisted we get to the trail.

"Hey, here's a map ... looks like it's six miles to the falls."

Greg checked his watch and looked to find the sun in the sky. "We've still got time. Let's do it."

"I was just thinking that Eugene couldn't possibly hike six miles, could he? Maybe they haven't gone to the falls."

"How about we'll just plan to go to the waterfall—if we see them along the way, we'll try to get more answers. If not, no worries, we will have had a very enjoyable afternoon." He smiled, pulled me in and gave me a quick kiss. "It's nice having some alone time with you."

I agreed. The afternoon was gorgeous and I have come to learn I adore being around this man.

We walked the mostly flat trail, only slowing down during segments where the trail turned to deep sand, which slowed our pace. There was no sign of either man along the way. We got to the falls and marveled how, in this desert terrain, there was a hundred-foot waterfall cascading down from stone formations and into a crystal-clear pool. It wasn't crowded, but there were other people already swimming. It looked cool and refreshing, but we hadn't planned for a swim—we hadn't even planned for a hike today—so we took our shoes and socks off and only went in knee high. Shadow bounded right on in, splashing anyone nearby. A couple kids next to us started squealing and playing with my pup, which got her even more excited. She ran out of the water, then turned quickly, sprinting back to it and then jumping in. She was in heaven.

Once we cooled down a little, we sat aside in the dirt watching Shadow continue to frolic in the water. She'd bite at the water, shake her head, jump out, spin around and run over to spray us with water, then she'd do it all over again. I hadn't laughed so hard in a long time, it seemed. We enjoyed the sun and forgot all about what led us to this spot. It was so nice to have some quiet time talking and laughing at the silly dog.

Greg had laid back in the sand and his eyes were closed. I checked my Fitbit—we had hiked six miles to get here and it took us an hour and a half. "We should get going since we don't have flashlights; sun will be setting in a couple hours."

Greg opened his eyes. "I guess it is getting late. Too bad we don't have a tent to just stay here all night. This is an amazing place."

"I think our friends would get worried," I leaned over and gave him a lingering kiss before we sat up to put our socks and shoes on.

"C'mon Shadow, get out of the water," I shouted,

before turning to Greg. "She's going to be a mess by the time we go back through all that sand."

Shadow came out, but her attention turned and was held opposite from where we were. At the far end of the swimming hole, two men had emerged on a trail that appeared from behind the rock formation. They both headed away from us on the trail. Shadow started barking and she ran off after them.

"Crap! Shadow is on the move," I yelled, as I quickly tied my shoelace and jumped up to chase her. "Shadow! Stop!"

My feet felt like they were stuck in mud as I struggled to go faster. The sand was fairly deep until I got to the far edge of the large swimming hole. I could still see Shadow ahead of me, but she appeared smaller by the second. She would be out of my sight in no time.

"Shadow!" Both Greg and I yelled in unison. He was running as fast as he could, too, but we both found it challenging.

I couldn't see my girl any longer and just prayed she stayed on the trail. For a nine-month-old pup, she was generally very good at not running off. However, she was still a puppy and I couldn't take anything for granted. I must catch up to her.

Finally, we made it to the trail and rounded the bend where we could see Shadow ahead. One man was on the ground, holding his ankle, with Shadow hovering right over him, barking in his face. He was swatting at her, but she was relentless. The other man was reaching for his friend just as I caught up.

Trying to catch my breath, I said, "Wh … what the hell? Eugene, what are you doing here?" I bent over, with my hands on my knees, breathing deep. Greg ran up and pulled Shadow back and clipped on her leash.

The grimace on the fallen man's face clearly stated the degree of pain he was in. As I knelt down, I saw that the beanie he wore covered brown and gray dreadlocks. This was the guy from Back Canyon Outfitters. I reached over, lifted up the cuff of his hiking pants, and flinched when I saw his leg. He was wearing short hiking shoes which easily showed the source of his pain. His ankle and lower leg were already purple and puffy.

"Greg, he's going to need help out of here." I began to gently touch in various spots. The man yelled out, cussing. "Yep, there's no way he's putting weight on this." I turned to the man, "What's your name?"

"Todd."

I tilted my head disbelieving. *I know that wasn't his name when he led us through the slot canyon.* Then remembered we had an emergency so I didn't question further. Greg moved away a few yards to make a phone call; he took Eugene with him and Shadow stuck close to the old man.

"Okay, Todd. We're going to help you get some medical attention. Do you have some water in that pack?" I indicated the knapsack that had been tossed aside. He nodded, and I grabbed his water and encouraged him to drink.

"This is all *that mutt's* fault!" he yelled, after drinking a sip.

I ignored him and pulled a shirt out of his pack and started to rip it in strips.

"Hey! What the hell are you doing?" Todd screamed, then fell to his side in pain.

"Todd, we're going to have to stabilize your leg in case we have to walk out of here." I remained calm, helping a man in need, even though my mind was racing and wondering how he knew Eugene. And, what were they doing out here specifically? How did a ninety-five-year-old man hike this far? All questions I would get answers to—later.

"Walk?" Todd could barely verbalize now. "We have a side-by-side—maybe half mile down the trail…" His face scrunched up in agony and he wrapped his arms around his chest, rocking gently until the pain subsided.

Greg and Eugene were already walking back to us.

"Eugene claims they got here by motorized vehicle," Greg stated.

"Yeah, that's what Todd was just telling me. I had no idea they were allowed on these trails. Did you already call for help?"

"Nope, couldn't get a connection. No signal."

"Okay, can you go see if you can locate the side-by-side?" Then, I turned to Todd. "Where's the key?"

He indicated his bag so I rummaged through, found it, and tossed it to Greg. "Also, can we look for some sticks or something to form a splint to stabilize this? Maybe Eugene could be working on that while you bring back the vehicle?"

Each man set out to do his job, while I tried to keep Todd calm. Daylight was diminishing, but with a motorized vehicle, I wasn't nearly as worried about the impending darkness. I was more worried about finding medical facilities for this guy. I was fairly confident that there wasn't anything in Boulder or Escalante. Perhaps Kanab. I guessed all these small towns should have volunteer fire departments, but I felt that he was going to require more help than that. Regardless, we'd move to where we found a cell connection and then call for help.

Eugene came back with some good sticks I could use

for a brace. With the strips of T-shirt and the sticks, I did the best job I could, trying to secure him for standing. I began to wonder what was taking Greg so long when I heard the engine.

The side-by side pulled up right next to us and Greg shut off the engine. "Well, it was more like a mile down the trail ... and disguised in some shrubbery pretty well. Sorry it took so long."

We both bent over and hoisted him up to a sitting position. Then we squatted just next to him, moving our shoulders into the space of Todd's underarms. Slowly, using all the strength we had in our legs, we raised from our squat. He was dead weight, but we assisted him up to standing on his good leg. We each adjusted our balance and caught our breath, then assisted him as we used our shoulders and upper bodies to stabilize his weight and hobble him the few feet over to the side-by-side. To keep the leg straight and elevated, we propped him up on the bench backseat. It wasn't elegant, but we managed through all the man's swearing. Shadow hunkered down on the floor below Todd where his feet would have been. The rest of us piled very tightly onto the front bench seat and Greg slowly drove us down the trail. With each bump and turn we could hear groans from the backseat.

Yelling over the engine noise, I needed information. "Eugene, how do you know Todd?"

"Oh, he's an in-law of mine," he said casually.

"What? And, you're just now telling us this?" Greg asked.

"We're all ears ... tell us the story, Eugene," I said.

CHAPTER THIRTEEN

It had been an excruciating journey to get back to the parking lot. Poor Todd was in so much pain and it didn't matter how slowly we tried to go; he couldn't get comfortable. The engine was too loud for Eugene to tell us his tales, so we opted for learning the whole story later. For now, we had to focus on getting the injured man some help.

We had cell service once we were back in the trailhead parking lot, so I called 911. By then, it was nearly six o'clock and we were exhausted and hungry. I also called Alexis to let the group back at the campground know that we were okay, but it would still be a while before we'd get back. Agatha was beyond worried about Eugene, I was told. I assured them that he was just fine and we'd fill them in on everything when we got back.

While we waited for the first responders to arrive, Todd started taunting Eugene.

"Your kids are behind all this, you know!" he hissed.

Eugene looked at him quizzically. "You don't know what you're talking about, son. I don't have children."

"That's your story."

I was curious where all this was going, so I just sat back listening. Greg also got very quiet as he sat back in the driver's seat of the side-by-side.

Eugene was calm and asked the simple question. "Who exactly do you think are my *children*?"

Todd grimaced while trying to raise his torso in his semi-sitting position. "Old man, you are crazy … you are dumb as rocks!"

I couldn't keep quiet any longer, "Hey! No name calling!" I scowled at Todd, and then looked to Eugene. "Why is he so adamant you have children? Is it possible you've never met them?"

Eugene shook his head. "This kid is the crazy one!" He sat down again on the passenger seat, twisting to look at Todd. "Who has told you this rubbish?"

Todd shrugged and appeared to be done with the accusations.

I tended to believe Eugene, since this guy had not been upfront with his identity. I decided no better time than the present to get some answers.

"Yesterday, you were introduced to us as Marley. Today, it's Todd. Which is it, mystery man?"

He glared at me, but immediately spat, "Marley's my outfitter's nickname. You know, the dreads…" he pulled on a braid, "Bob Marley?"

I rolled my eyes.

"I know, it's stupid … but that's what the guys call me."

We all turned when we heard the vehicles making their way along the dusty road.

"Finally!" Greg exclaimed. He got up and waved his arms in the air to lead them over to where we were.

After the EMTs took his vitals, they got Todd out of the side-by-side and onto a stretcher. They removed my makeshift splint, and evaluated the injury closer. Within a few minutes, they took Greg aside.

"We're taking him to the county hospital in Kanab. That's the closest we've got, but don't worry, we just gave him a sedative so his pain should subside in a bit."

"Thank you for your help." Greg shook the guy's hand and then turned to Todd. "Hey man, should we follow you guys in your truck?"

He was already groggy. "Uh, can you ... mmm, can you park the side-by-side on the trailer? Then call the outfitter place in the morning. They'll come pick it up—they have keys."

"Sure. Not a problem." Greg took the keys Todd offered and hurried off. The EMTs began to load him into the ambulance while Greg maneuvered the vehicles before returning.

"All locked up. Here are your keys," he told Todd, and then handed them to the closest rescuer. "We'll check on you in the morning."

"Thanks. Oh, and get the old man to tell you what he's been up to! He's up to no good ... he's squandering my father's inheritance!" he yelled as the EMTs closed up the doors. They got in the vehicle and pulled out of the parking lot.

Turning to me, Greg and I stared at each other in disbelief. Greg looked concerned, "Where's Eugene?" he asked.

"Sitting in his truck. May be sleeping now for all I know." I was concerned for a different reason—forget about the stupid supposed treasures. "Did you find any family member to call for Todd?"

"Nope, he said there's no one. But, I'm going to call the outfitter place to let them know what happened and to pick up these vehicles. Hopefully, they'll help him."

Suddenly I felt a sadness wash over me. "Should we be following them to the hospital?"

"Libby, there's nothing more we can do tonight. Like I told the guy, we'll call tomorrow and check on him. For now, let's get back to the campground. I'm starving, and I doubt there's anything still open in that small town …"

"Oh!" I interjected. "Alexis said they grilled ribs tonight. There's still plenty." His eyes lit up and that's all the motivation we needed to make the final leg of our journey. "I'll drive the Jeep. Why don't you drive Eugene's truck back? I don't feel good about him driving, it's been quite the day."

Alexis turned out to be our guardian angel. When we pulled up, she had already reheated and laid out a spread of food that immediately had me drooling. BBQ ribs, potato salad, baked beans, and some cheddar biscuits. Eugene, Greg, and I each immediately filled our plates with loads of food, grabbed a beer, and sat at the picnic table. You'd have thought that we had hiked for days the way we were quickly consuming everything.

"We were starting to get worried about you," JJ said. "Thanks for calling us earlier so we knew not to send the sheriff out looking."

Agatha was picking at her teeth with a toothpick.

"Yeah, I just wish I'd known *you* had met up with *them*." She pointed from Eugene and then to the two of us sitting next to him. "I was worried sick. *Again*."

Eugene used a napkin to wipe his mouth, and then stated calmly, "Agatha. You just need to relax. I've been exploring all my life and I don't need help." She glared at him and then took a drink of her beer.

"Speaking of which, Eugene … earlier, you were about to tell us all about finding this in-law of yours. We'd like to know—where'd you meet up with Todd?" I asked.

Agatha looked confused. "Todd? Who the hell is Todd?"

Eugene took a sip of his beer and then set it down. He pushed aside his empty plate, leaned back slightly, then maneuvered his legs out from under the picnic table. He slowly stood and made his way over to one of the zero-gravity reclining chairs just near me. Once he got settled, he started in on his story.

"You all may not know, but I was married a time or two before Agatha here," he pointed to her. "My previous wife's name was Evelyn Lee. We were married for twenty some odd years before the good Lord took her. There were promises I made to her that I'm still trying to fulfill."

I sensed Agatha's impatience as she shifted in her seat before she ultimately retreated to their camper. My heart went out to her. It seemed to me that she had long lived in the shadow of this former wife. That had to be difficult.

"Evelyn had a brother…" Eugene continued the whole tale of Evelyn's family tree and we learned that Walter was her brother. This must be the one who Agatha mentioned. Eugene told story after story about all the philanthropic work her brother had done and how respected he was in his community.

After about half an hour, I realized he was still rambling on about Walter, but that he still had not answered my question related to the injured man we met today—Todd. I could see that everyone's eyes were heavy and I wanted to spur this conversation along.

"So, Eugene, is Todd one of Evelyn's relatives then?"

"Oh! Yeah. He was one of Walter's sons. He's the youngest of five and we had never met the boy, but heard all kinds of stories about him."

He proceeded for the next hour to explain how Walter's son had always been trouble, but now that he's in his fifties, he's settled down some. Todd and his father had been at war with one another and then when dad passed away, he learned that all the hidden treasures were probably still out there just waiting to be found. Eugene noticed him after the third city they'd traveled to since leaving home on this trip nearly a month ago. This same guy kept turning up in the same places and he needed to figure out why. When they were at Lake Powell, he discovered the man actually worked for an outfitter near Kanab ... so he called up and booked him for a slot canyon hike. Eugene knew that Agatha was already getting perturbed with his and Evelyn's obsession, so he just wanted to quietly go out and do this one thing on his own. That's when he first learned that Todd was related to his former wife. He told us it excited him to meet this long-lost relative and he wanted to get to know him better. They took the RV to boondock for a night on state land—or what's commonly known as *dispersed* camping, just outside of town—that's when Todd tried to convince Eugene that he had a daughter looking for him too. He felt it was a warning, more so than delivering happy news of a long-lost child. But, Eugene was convinced—he did not have any children.

Everyone in our group, but me, had drifted off to sleep in their chairs as Eugene kept on going. Shadow and I were mesmerized by this elderly man—his energy, tenacity, and strong will was amazing. Even though he had frustrated me several times since we'd met, I found him enchanting and I felt so grateful he'd come into our lives. There was a nagging that lingered in my brain—most things in life happen for a reason. Was there a higher meaning to these two entering our lives right now? I wasn't sure what that could possibly be, but the excitement stirring within me concluded that I wouldn't stop until I figured it out.

"Well, looks like I've bored everyone to sleep," Eugene stated, as he struggled to get out of the comfortable weight-defying chair. "We should probably all go get some shut eye. It'll be a big day tomorrow."

"Wait. What's tomorrow?" I asked.

"Thursday."

"No, I mean, what are your plans for tomorrow?"

"It's the day we learn what all this has been about!" He produced a huge smile and walked off to his trailer.

CHAPTER FOURTEEN

Eugene's last statement about 'figuring it all out' ran on repeat through my brain all night long. I found that I wanted to be part of this treasure hunt even though I was fairly confident the rest of our group would not. Maybe that *is* the higher purpose ... it could be that *I'm* meant to help this man keep his deathbed promise to the love of his life? Maybe our paths crossed because this is my dharma? We keep running into Eugene and Agatha for a reason! And then I remembered the warning that Todd had delivered to us ... *ask the old man what he's been up to?*

I hopped right out of bed, leaving Greg with his dreams. Shadow came crawling out of her spot under the dining table and joined me in the extremely cramped bathroom. She always follows me to the bathroom. I guess this is what most moms feel like—at least my sister, Jordan, has told me how she's never been able to pee alone since having her menagerie of children. Shadow's tail started wagging, slapping the side walls, and making a horrific bang. Poor Greg, trying to sleep in the next room.

Shadow bounded out of the bathroom once I was done and we hurried to get her bra and leash attached. She was definitely indicating the need for 'out.' The second we stepped into the cool morning air, I saw that Eugene and Agatha had left. *Of course, they had!* Shadow pulled me right over to their site, where she sniffed around, did her business, and then led me right back to our RV. She sat just off the bottom step leading into the camper and pointed her nose up to the frosted window in the door. A note.

I pulled it from the window. It read: **Headed to CC. Thank you all for everything. Best, A&E**

Despite momentary disappointment, at least they learned one thing from us—tell people where you're going! I smiled, folded the paper and put it in my shorts pocket. "C'mon Shadow. First, I've gotta go pick up your mess over there. Then, I think we both need a longer walk." Shadow seemed to agree. I grabbed a poop bag and we headed out again.

As we walked around the campground, I found that it was still quite early—six a.m. What time did those two head out? We were up really late. Maybe it's true that as you age, you sleep less? I don't want to get old, I decided. I love my sleep too much. The low light of the morning sky was gorgeous. The birds were just starting to chirp and getting busy finding food. There was a light breeze which made me wish I had put on a jacket. No, scratch that; I was reveling in the coolness that we hadn't seen in Mesa since April. I was dreading going back. In late September, you'd think it would be cool there, but it wasn't until sometime in November that we really felt the distinct change in seasons.

As we walked up our row of trailers, I saw Alexis out, stretching on her yoga mat so we stopped.

"I see our friends left early," she said as we approached.

"Did you hear when they left?" I asked.

"I think I may have heard an engine around four?"

"Wow, we didn't even go to bed until after midnight."

I pulled the note from my pocket and handed it to Lexi. She had the same sentiment—at least this time they left an explanation. I suppose they didn't even owe us that. But, on the other hand, we all had started to become close as we shared these experiences together. I wondered if we would run into them ever again? We had each other's phone numbers so hopefully that meant we'd keep in touch.

"Are we still planning on hiking Bryce Canyon today?" Alexis asked.

"That's what Greg and JJ were discussing yesterday. I think they were planning on searching online for RV reservations this morning. We'll see."

Just then JJ appeared from their camper with coffee mug in hand. It reminded me that I hadn't had my first cup. I left Shadow with them and ran off to make me a cup. When I returned, JJ was telling Lexi more about the conversation with Agatha from the day before.

"Yeah, I swear she said Eugene has kids of his own, but doesn't have a relationship with them."

"Really?" I asked as I took a seat next to him. "How'd that come up then?"

"I guess this newly found in-law was getting under her skin. She said it in a way that I took it to mean *you pay more attention to this guy than your own kids*." JJ took a sip of coffee, shook his head slightly, then stated, "I really enjoy this couple—but, I'm at a loss to figure them out. They're interesting. I feel particularly drawn to him; she's a bit rough at times, but then again, I kinda feel for her."

"Precisely my same thoughts…" I started to laugh. "She's funny in a lot of ways, but then I wonder if that's the intent or are we laughing at something that is actually tragic. Can you imagine keeping up with Eugene all the time?"

Alexis snorted, nearly drowning herself in coffee. "Oh geez. All over me!" She coughed and reached for a nearby towel. Dabbing at the coffee dripping down her front, she started to giggle. "No, I cannot imagine. Their life is so different from mine. Ours." She collectively pointed around our group. "Who spends all their time on the road in search of something that might not even be?"

JJ nodded in agreement. "But, there's part of me that is envious of them. When we are no longer working full-time jobs, what will we be doing? You can't deny that they are actually getting out there and living. Even though their way of doing things seems unconventional, they are certainly living … traveling, meeting people, dancing … sheesh, more than we do most weeks!"

"True. I'm a bit envious, I have to admit," I added.

"I suppose." Alexis continued drinking her coffee, while JJ explored his own thoughts about why he was drawn to the elderly man.

He started sharing more about stuff he'd found online related to his own ancestry.

"But, JJ…" I was skeptical, but wanted to be respectful of my friend, "just because you never knew your mother, doesn't mean Eugene even knew your mother, much less had children with her. You know that, right?"

JJ looked a tad wounded. "Of course, Libby. Have you ever just had a strong gut instinct about something before, though?"

I had to think about that. There were moments I could recount feeling intuitive. Of course, nothing of this magnitude. To just randomly think that someone you just met could be related? No.

"I guess I really haven't experienced that, JJ." I was still curious though. "What exactly do you think is similar?"

"Well, for instance, our blue eyes." He leaned over and opened his eyes extra wide for me to see. Alexis burst out laughing. I leaned in and examined his irises.

"Hmmm. Ok, I suppose." I glanced at Alexis and winked. "What else?"

"Ok. His love of hunting!"

Alexis set down her mug, then leaned in with both her elbows on her knees, interlacing her fingers. "Hon, we've been married now for eight years. You've gone hunting *maybe* twice in that whole time. How is that similar?"

"Ok. Well, then … his height! He is tall. I am tall. He's originally from Wyoming and so am I!"

Alexis chuckled to herself as I jumped back in. "Sure. Those are things … yes. However, I think we really need more. His last name is Walker. Yours is Johnson. Did you take on your mother's or father's last name?"

That stumped him. "I guess I've always thought Johnson was my father's last name. Heather's maiden name was Thompson."

Gently, Alexis touched her husband's knee. "Sweetie, your mom is actually your stepmom, remember? I know you've been super close for over forty years, but she isn't your blood relative."

He hung his head. "There's no way he could be my long-lost father, could he?"

"Probably not," she answered calmly.

"It's okay to research your family history, JJ…" I felt bad killing his excitement. "Just try to manage your expectation. He probably isn't related, but it's fantastic that you've met a new friend regardless." I reached out and gave his hand a little squeeze.

Greg walked up to us with that same confused expression we'd already had this morning, and pointing to the vacant site. Alexis handed him the note.

"Ahhh. So, I guess this clears the way for us to hike Bryce Canyon today!" he exclaimed.

CHAPTER FIFTEEN

It was around noon when we pulled away from Escalante, headed toward Bryce Canyon. It was only an hour's journey and I was very excited to get out of the desert and up into the forest. We were hoping for accommodations for two RVs for the next couple nights, but so far weren't successful in securing that. Hope is generally not a strategy, but in this case, we were still holding out hope that someone's last minute cancellations would work in our favor.

Over the two-way radio, I said laughing, "Breaker, breaker one nine, gotta copy?"

Laughter was all I got back. Then, "Since when do you speak *trucker*?" Alexis said continuing to crack up.

"I suppose those old Smokey and the Bandit reruns?" I have no idea where I get half the stuff I say. "Hey, looks like Ruby's is just up ahead—wanna pull in for lunch?"

"10-4," she laughed even louder than before.

The temperatures outside were still fairly mild. We made sure to leave the RV windows open for fresh air. Shadow hadn't even raised her head from her place under the table as we stepped out.

My friend Alexis was still laughing and carrying on at my expense when we all unloaded from our separate vehicles and walked toward the restaurant.

"I just love you, Libby Madsen," she said, giving me a huge hug. "I'm having so much fun on this vacation. Seems like something new to laugh about *every single day*. Just what we needed, huh?"

We followed the guys into the restaurant, with masks on. There weren't many people, but we were thankful they were serving lunch, as we had not eaten breakfast before we packed up and left.

We ordered our food and then I excused myself from the table. Walking into the ladies restroom, I could see that the far stall was taken. I settled into the first one. Within seconds, I found myself oddly interested in a loud conversation. The female's voice sounded irritated. "He's just a stupid old man! Why can't you just get him to tell you where it is?" It must have been something she said that made me think she was also talking to a man, but I couldn't be certain. I sat there listening longer than I would have because, well, I was mesmerized by the conversation and also, *who talks on their phone on the toilet?* She yelled at the person on the other end, "You were supposed to be here *last night*!" It was evident the person's answer was not good enough. "I want whatever you found in that … whatever the hell you call it…*monolith*… and I want it NOW!"

Following that scream, she slammed through the stall door and exited the bathroom.

Ewww. She didn't even wash her hands!

Now I was super curious so I rushed through washing my hands, left the bathroom, and nearly ran down the short hallway back into the dining room. Stopping abruptly, I looked left. Then, I looked right. The only people I saw was our group and then an older couple at a table across the room. The woman seated there didn't appear at all like she had just hurried back into place. She didn't appear upset or anything. Suddenly I felt silly. What was I doing? I casually walked by the glass front doors on the way back to our table and glanced outside. I didn't see anyone, but there was a large lifted blue pickup squealing its tires, leaving the parking lot. I had remembered seeing it as we pulled in earlier; it was parked just to the south of us.

Greg looked at me curiously as I took my seat, and asked, "Whatcha looking for out there? Worried about Shadow?"

"Oh, no." I waved it off, then laughed. "Did you guys see a girl run out of the restaurant? A lady in one of the bathroom stalls was having quite the conversation. Yelling. But, what was strange about it, and why I wanted to see who she was ... she mentioned something about a monolith. Could it be the one we saw near White Pocket?"

Greg thought about it for a second, but before he could respond, the food arrived and we all became distracted as salads, burgers, and wraps were placed in front of us. After several bites, Alexis spoke up, "You asked if we saw someone leave? I saw some guy come from that direction. Little taller than you, heavier, and wearing a green ball cap. Didn't see a girl, though. He went straight outside, but I did notice that he shoved open those glass doors quite strongly. I was worried they'd smash into the wall."

I wondered where she had gone. I know the voice was that of a female … how old, couldn't be sure. I kept thinking young, like teenager or early twenties at most. But, who knows, voices are tricky. Anyway, it wasn't important. I was being nosey again.

Once our plates had been removed from the table, JJ pulled out his iPad. Our waitress came back by to bring our check and noticed he was on the campground reservations site. "Won't find anythang for tonight. People's made reservations months ago," she informed. "Gotta go to Panguitch. Just down the road."

I'd heard of Panguitch. How had I heard of Panguitch? I couldn't remember. "Thank you!" Once she walked off, I turned to JJ. "Any places available there?" He began to look it up.

Alexis sat back in her seat, grimacing. "I'm stuffed now. Hiking no longer sounds fun."

"I was thinking the same thing. Maybe we go get settled in a town close by, then we'll hit the trails early tomorrow morning?" I suggested. Everyone agreed and we headed out of the restaurant and back to the RVs.

While I walked Shadow around, JJ found us a place at Panguitch Lake which sounded nice. Apparently, the town was only thirty miles farther on Hwy 12, so we loaded up and headed on down the road.

CHAPTER SIXTEEN

We'd been on the road for five nights so far. We still had more than a week before we had to be back in Arizona. There was so much we still wanted to do, but I couldn't help but be distracted by all the talk of treasures and valuables. No, I didn't care about finding these things for my own benefit; I really wanted to help Eugene fulfill his promise. Why was this suddenly so important to me? I had a fondness for the man and I suppose I just wanted to see that he finished this search before his time was up. Oh well. Not much I could do about that now—they had ventured on and I needed to get my head back into our own group's plans.

Settled in at Panguitch Lake for two nights, we enjoyed a lazy afternoon, fishing off of paddle boats we'd rented. The weather was perfect—not too hot, slightly chilly but nothing a light jacket wouldn't help.

"I saw an old-fashioned ice cream shop as we passed through town," I told Greg. His eyes lit up at the mention. I shouted over to our friends who were several yards away from us on the lake. "Lexi—wanna get ice cream?" Both her and JJ's heads quickly flipped toward us, their eyebrows raised excitedly as they started paddling fast toward shore. "I guess that means yes!" We got our feet moving and paddled to catch up with our friends, racing them in the end and beating them to shore.

I licked the blackberry vanilla drips that were melting down the side of my warm waffle cone. We walked along the main street of Panguitch toward a small arts and crafts fair. I pulled off to the side under a shade tree and gave Shadow more of her own small dairy-free peanut butter 'ice cream'. She licked a couple times and then engulfed the scoop in one mouthful. "Whoa! Well, that's that then. No more." She looked up at me as though I'd share mine. "No way! C'mon, let's keep going."

We wandered around the booths at the fair. I was admiring some local artists' jewelry when I got a tap on the shoulder. "Howdy there, pal!" I turned to find Agatha behind me.

"Well, look at that! What are you guys doing here?" I gave her a hug, looking around for Eugene.

"Apparently, we got distracted again," she rolled her eyes laughing. "Where y'all staying?"

"We were supposed to be in Bryce Canyon…"

"Yeah, that's what I thought!"

"No campsites available. So, we came here." My hand

fanned out indicating the park we were in. I scanned the area again and didn't see my friends or Eugene. "Hey, I thought you guys were headed to Cedar City?"

"RV is having some problems and there's a mechanic right down the road."

"Ohhh. That sucks, I'm sorry."

We started walking down the path between concession stands. Agatha sighed heavily, "I'm worried about Eugene," she stated.

I stopped and turned to her. "Why? What happened?"

"Something is really weighing on his mind. He won't really talk about it, but he did say something about Walter's son…"

"Todd?"

"Yes! Apparently, when they went out following a clue, he told Eugene that his kids are one step ahead of them. That's why we're not finding what Walter hid!"

"Does he have kids?" I asked.

"No!"

"He talked about having been married several times. Is it *possible*? Even if he didn't know about them?"

"Well…" she seemed to contemplate for several moments. "His first wife—she was a real piece of work."

"How?"

"She was a player. At least from what he's told me of her—which isn't much! She was a scammer. A gold digger, and up to no good. Of course, he didn't say that. He always sees the best in everyone. I gathered that just reading between the lines."

"So, you think she could have gotten pregnant and didn't tell him?"

"I don't think you could rule it out."

"But, if she was a gold digger, wouldn't she have come after him for money?"

"He didn't have any way back then."

Ah. Good point. None of us have money when we're young.

"Okay. Let's just say she got pregnant and he didn't know before they split up. Why now … what brings the kids out of the woodwork now?"

"I don't know."

Of course. My question really was rhetorical. If they knew, then they'd be telling that story instead, wouldn't they? My guess is that he's ninety-five and surely, they are coming out of the woodwork in time for his demise. Lovely.

I caught sight of Greg, JJ, and Eugene sitting on a park bench. We walked over to them.

Greg smiled. "Hey, I see you found the better half where you were!"

Agatha looked appreciative of the compliment. "And, Eugene found his buddies!"

"Where's Alexis?" I asked

"She went back to the booth selling pottery. She was after a small piece she thought would be a nice gift for her mother-in-law." Greg then turned to JJ. "Your mother doing okay with Joshua now five days in?"

He nodded. "They are having a great time. Not so sure about my father. He's not used to the littles being around."

Greg laughed and nodded in agreement. "I bet it is something to get used to."

Eugene piped up, "Hey kids, why don't we all go to that steakhouse for dinner tonight? The one on the main drag. My treat!"

The rest of us glanced amongst each other and shrugged *why not*. "Sure, that sounds great! But, really, you don't need to treat us," I answered.

"No, I insist. You've saved my bacon a couple times and I'd like to buy you dinner."

"Okay, then. We'd love to join you guys!"

"I'll make reservations for seven," Agatha added.

* * *

Dinner was delicious. It had been quite some time since I'd had a full steak meal at a restaurant. I pushed my plate away once I finished, put my mask back on, and excused myself. I had been drinking so much water on this trip, I felt like I was the only one always excusing myself to go to the bathroom.

No one was in there when I entered. I chose the middle stall. Was there a strategy that women used for choosing? Mine seemed to be to veer away from the first stall, when at all possible, as it's probably the one that gets used the most. The second I had latched the door, I heard someone else enter the room.

"Tell the old man he's getting dangerously close," an ominous warning, delivered by a female's voice.

"Excuse me?" I shouted.

"Ask him to pass the salt." The door slammed.

I rushed to get out, but missed whoever ran off.

Greg noticed that I was bothered when I got back to the table. "What's wrong?" he quietly asked me.

I looked over to Eugene who was full of smiles as he talked with JJ.

"Hon, I don't think Eugene is safe," I whispered.

"Why?"

"I'll tell you more later…" Alexis had already turned away from her conversation with Agatha and heard me. Now, the whole table looked over to me.

"Tell us what?" she asked. I took a sip of my water and just shook my head to dismiss that there was anything to share.

When everyone was engaged again in conversation, I found myself looking around the restaurant. There were several small groups spread throughout the dining room, but it wasn't crowded. The voice in the bathroom sounded familiar, but I couldn't place it. One thing for sure, someone had *followed* me in. We were being followed … targeted. Why?

I tuned back into the conversation just in time to hear Eugene telling JJ that they still planned on heading over to Cedar City the next day. That is, if their RV was finished. The repair shop indicated it would be midday tomorrow and then they'd set out.

Agatha was informing Alexis that the cousins they were going to see owned a goat farm. She was excited to get some cheese and milk from them. And, she was thankful to take a couple days off from the 'treasure travel' and instead just visit with family. After that, she said they'd head up to Salt Lake City.

"Hey, Eugene," I interrupted. "Did you check in at the hospital about Todd?"

"Yeah. Sounds like he's got himself a fracture. A pilon fracture. So, he's in a walking boot now. It compresses to keep the injury from getting worse. He's supposed to keep it elevated as much as possible for several weeks, but he'll be okay. His boss picked up the truck and trailer. He said all was good."

"Oh, thank goodness."

"What were you guys doing out there on that trail anyway?" Greg asked.

Eugene leaned in, and the rest of us followed his lead. In a quieter voice, he began the story of Todd approaching him back in Kanab. The clues Eugene thought he was following for years now—Southwest, Salton Sea, and Big Fish—were being challenged by Todd. At first, Eugene didn't understand how this young man from the excursion company knew him. That was quickly answered when he produced identification that proved he was Walter's errant son, the one he'd never met.

He went on to explain that Todd had found coins hidden in a secret compartment of the shiny metal monolith located out in the desert wilderness near White Pocket. Our whole group exchanged knowing glances.

"That's why we had to venture out that night—to meet up with him. Only Todd never showed and we couldn't find it," Agatha explained.

"The next day, I got another call from the young man," Eugene started.

Greg interrupted, "Todd? He's not that young, is he? I was thinking fifties…"

Eugene just grinned, "Son, everyone is young to me."

We all laughed; he definitely had a point.

"Anyway, I arranged with Todd for him to take me out the next day … that's when he took me to Escalante."

"The slot canyon hike…" I remembered.

"Right. He kept rambling on about these clues he swears his father told him about … and different from the ones I had."

He went on to explain that Todd dropped him off in an area where he was sure to find what he was looking for. Eugene hiked along a trail for four or five hours, to find nothing. Eugene waited with a Bureau of Land Management agent for some time in the parking lot, waiting for his ride to return. By the time that Todd returned, it was quite late. Eugene explained that Todd seemed very put out, but they stopped off at a convenience store anyway, and that's when he found the RV sitting there. Eugene still had his set of RV keys with him so that's when they set out for some dispersed camping. He indicated they had a real nice night, just talking. Todd went on to explain that some girl he used to date had told him she was Eugene Walker's daughter. Of course, Todd had known from his own family, he knew 'Eugene Walker' had married his aunt. That started a search for the man—he wanted to team up to find the family loot together. Simple as that.

"So, he had left you to do this hike, and then you trusted him again when he took you out to the falls?" Greg surmised.

He nodded. "Yes. He wanted to show me another spot he'd found."

"Wait, had you intended to do that slot canyon hike alone? Or was it a surprise that he left you?"

"He got a call from the boss about a new reservation. He had to go, but I wanted to stay. He said he'd be back."

"That must have been the reservation we made with that company … he had to guide our hike," JJ interjected. "Did you guys recognize him as our guide from that day?" he asked Greg and me.

I nodded. "Yeah, that's why we went over to Back Canyon Outfitters that afternoon in Escalante. We didn't remember his name, but we definitely recognized him. We wanted to see if they'd picked up Eugene. Shadow definitely recognized the guy; he was so shady with us that we ultimately played as though we *didn't* recognize him because we hoped he'd open up to us. That didn't work either—he recognized us."

Alexis said out loud what all of us were thinking, "Eugene, it seems to me like he didn't expect you to come back from that slot canyon adventure." We all turned to stare at her. "Well, who leaves a ninety-five-year-old out in the middle of the desert on his own?"

Suddenly, I wondered if Todd had something to do with the bathroom warning.

CHAPTER SEVENTEEN

Once we were back at our RV, I turned on the TV for some background noise. Quietly, I sat next to Greg at the dining table.

"What do you make of the stories Eugene told tonight?" I asked him.

"Oh, where to start," he sighed. "I gotta be honest. There's a whole lot those two tell that I'm convinced could be dementia. But, then you did find some coins. And those clues…"

"I know!" I got excited. "I'm going through the same thoughts. And, *why* do I feel so compelled to know more?"

"Hey, when you came back from the bathroom tonight, you said you had something to tell me."

"Oh gosh! Nearly forgot." I took a large sip of water. "A woman spooked me … gave a warning."

"What warning?" he got defensive.

"*Tell the old man he's getting dangerously close.*" Before he could respond, I remembered the other bit. "Also, she told me to ask him to *pass the salt.*"

"What on earth?" His face showed concern. "Libby, I don't want you to go into anymore restrooms alone. Ask Alexis to go with you."

"I was thinking the same thing. And," I got quieter and leaned in, "this also means that someone is following us."

* * *

In the Johnson's camper, JJ was consumed by Ancestry. com again. Alexis cozied up in a corner of the couch with a book. After the third 'hmmm…' from JJ, she put her book down and asked, "Finding anything?"

"I'm not sure. All this is very confusing, plus I just wonder if this really works. But, I learned that my grandparents originally settled in Texas, before living most of their adult lives in Wyoming. I could only find information on my mother's maternal side of the family. I was always told my mother's maiden name was Smith, but I'm unsure what her mother's maiden name was, and do you realize how common a name Smith is? And then, I'm completely lost on my grandfather's side of the family. Guess I need to ask my dad some more questions when we get home."

"I think it's great you are interested in all this. This is the most that I've even heard you mention your biological mother's side of the family at all. I'm so used to Heather being 'mom' that it sounds strange to hear you talk about anyone else."

"I do, too. Heather had always been there as a mother

for me—from my earliest memories anyway."

"Do you know what happened to your bio mom?"

"I know that she ran around on my dad a lot. He's made mention of that. There are stories that her upbringing wasn't the greatest either; she got caught up with the wrong crowd. Dad never could get her to settle down, apparently—I mean they were very young. She couldn't handle being a mother and signed all rights to me and my sister over to Dad."

"Do you know if she's still alive?"

He shrugged. "Dunno. And, I'm not sure if anyone does. She pretty much vanished."

Alexis stood behind JJ while he sat at the dining room table. She squeezed his shoulders and started massaging his neck. "I'm sorry, hon. That has to weigh on you at times…"

"Honestly, Dad and Heather did such a great job raising us, I barely think about the fact that my supposed 'real' mom was never there."

"I agree, they raised two beautiful and very responsible children—they should be very proud. Has Rene ever mentioned wanting to find her mother?" Rene was JJ's older sister, who lived in Boston.

"We've never talked about it, but I would like to get together with her sometime soon. Maybe there's more I could learn from her perspective? She's older … maybe she remembers more?"

Alexis went back to her book. JJ continued researching online until bedtime.

* * *

We had all agreed we'd head up the mountain to Bryce Canyon early the next morning. By the time we arrived at the visitor's center, the sun was just making its debut above the forested horizon. The first shuttle was leaving at six a.m.

"Glad we layered up. It's kind of chilly this morning!" Greg said, as we unloaded our packs from the car. He ran in to pay our park entrance fees and secure the permits for the backcountry hike.

JJ and Alexis shoved a few water bottles into their packs and clipped the stainless-steel water containers to their waistbands. I gave Shadow a drink of water before clipping on her leash, then we all headed over to the shuttle stop. Without previous reservations for overnight camping, they highly encouraged day visitors to take the free shuttles instead. Today we planned to complete the 8.8-mile Riggs Spring Loop. It would take us all day; the elevation changes were quite aggressive, but we were up for the challenge.

Being the only ones on the shuttle this early, Shadow hopped up onto the seat and panted as she looked out the window. The day was overcast, chilly, but not cold—perfect for some rigorous exercise. It wasn't long before we were dropped off at the trailhead. We hefted our packs up onto our shoulders and set out, letting Greg and JJ set the pace for the group.

Alexis and I talked more about JJ's newfound interest in his family's background. "I think that meeting Eugene has spurred this interest. I wonder if he'll actually talk to his dad about it when we return. They aren't that type of family, really. I see his dad as the type who is all buttoned up and doesn't express feelings."

"You know, I understand where JJ is coming from.

With Eugene anyway," I started breathing heavier as the incline increased. Finally with more oxygen in the lungs, I continued, "It sounds weird, and maybe it's just the fact that I miss my father, but ever since we met the man, I want to protect him. I actually *worry* about him."

"That's just because you are *you*, Libby," Alexis laughed. "You feel empathy for *everything* and *everyone* around you. Remember that lizard Shadow killed a month or so ago? I've never seen anyone cry over a dead lizard!"

"Oh, the poor thing." I had forgotten about that horrible day. I turned to her and stuck out my bottom lip in sorrow.

"See!" She laughed again. Then, once we both caught our breath as the terrain leveled again, she continued, "You and JJ are similar that way with Eugene. He must be triggering some parental loss for both of you. JJ losing his mother at a young age and you were so close to your father before he passed. The teen years are brutal enough; I can't imagine also losing a parent during that time."

We realized we weren't keeping pace with the guys so we sped it up a bit. Then I told Alexis about my encounters at Ruby's and at the steakhouse last night.

"What? Why didn't you tell me this yesterday?"

"I didn't really want to say anything in front of Eugene and Agatha. Even though I do believe this person has to be following us because of them, I … well, I guess I have that feeling I need to protect them."

"Weren't they heading to Cedar City today?" she asked.

"If their RV gets fixed in time." I took a drink from my water canister. "Speaking of their RV—do you think they're safe in that thing? It's got to be forty years old!"

"Libby, I don't go around worrying myself over such

things. You need to let it go. Think about it—if we'd never met them, you wouldn't be worried right now."

I laughed. My friend was so right.

"Now, what you should be worried about is not their RV, but that dark message about the old man getting dangerously close." She stopped, turned to me, and took my arm. "*That's* something to worry about. And, sure, we didn't know them a week ago, but now we do, so we probably should warn them about *that*."

"You're right. I'll call them when we get back into civilization." Shadow pulled me to go faster; she realized we'd lost the guys. We sped up again and caught them just as they were removing their packs for a small break.

The rest of the day went about the same. We struggled through elevation changes, went faster along the level sections, watched our footing on the downhill terrain, and took frequent breaks to recover. All things considered, the eight-mile hike went relatively fast. It was two in the afternoon by the time we loaded back onto another shuttle to the visitor center parking lot. Our legs ached, sweat dripped off our bodies, and our hiking clothes were soaked through, but all of us agreed that we'd plan a future five-night backcountry packing adventure and complete the full thirty-two-mile trek. It was stunning country and each of us was reluctant to leave.

"Shadow did great!" I exclaimed between gulps of water. "Wish I had four legs." Shadow was at my feet, looking up and panting hard.

JJ removed his hat and wiped the top of his close-cropped blonde head with a small towel. "She did better than most of us. Dang, that last section was hard, wasn't it?"

Alexis nodded vigorously. "I'm starting to get famished now. No more protein bars and fruit, I want something substantial."

"By the time we get off this mountain, it'll be a good time for a beer!" Greg added, "I'm up for early dinner."

JJ was already looking up the options in Panguitch. "There aren't that many choices ... but I see a grill that looks okay. Burgers, sandwiches, salads ... oh, and, beer!"

"Are we going to eat first then head out to the lake campground?" I asked. "Or, go in looking like this."

"Uh, let's just go eat..." Greg suggested. "Once I shower, I'm probably done for."

We all agreed.

CHAPTER EIGHTEEN

Eugene and Agatha's RV wasn't fixed yet, I learned when I called them. We had already eaten our early dinner, but I invited them to join us out at the lake. Arriving just prior to sunset, they set their chairs out by us and we enjoyed watching the calm lake and all its wildlife. It was very quiet, hardly any other campers around. Shadow immediately planted herself at Eugene's feet and then stared up at him with adoration.

We told them all about our Bryce Canyon hike. They had driven their truck over to Cedar City for the day to visit with their relatives and hoped by the time they got back that their RV would be ready.

JJ sat closest to Eugene and was engaged in conversation with him. Alexis, Greg, and I got an earful from Agatha.

"The cousins were sure of it!" Agatha exclaimed when

telling us about asking them whether Eugene had children with his wife.

"You mean, they were certain he did *not* have children with his first wife?" I clarified.

"Yep, that's what I said."

Greg was puzzled. "I don't understand why Todd was so adamant about it then. How would he know anyway? It's not as though he was ever close to the guy."

Agatha just shook her head. "He's sketchy." She pulled her toothpick out of her shirt pocket and started picking her teeth.

I nodded my head in agreement. I felt bad he got hurt, but yes, something was very sketchy about that guy. What was he up to?

JJ shouted over to us to get our attention. "Hey guys, he and his first wife lived in Wyoming—next door to her parents!" He smiled, then dived back into Eugene's story.

Greg and I looked at each other, confused. Alexis quietly explained to Greg. "I think he wants to believe that Eugene is related … grandfather or something? He's been spending each evening on Ancestry.com doing research."

"Really?" he asked. "I mean, looking at them side by side, they're both tall and lean in stature. Both have crystal blue eyes. By the looks of Eugene's fine white hair, I assume he was also blonde in his youth. And, their fair skin … physically, I could see them being related. But, that's just silly. Isn't it?" I laughed it off.

"I'm not sure what's going on with him lately. He has gotten on this kick about needing to know where he comes from. He never knew his mother so there are a lot of questions swirling around in that brain."

Greg asked, "Couldn't he ask his father?"

"I don't know. He's not very open about that time in his life. I get the feeling that once he met Heather, he erased everything else. Almost as though the family unit—JJ, Rene, Heather, and him—were the only family of his."

Agatha changed subject abruptly. "Where are you guys headed next? You check out of here tomorrow, right?"

I looked to Alexis to make sure she was finished talking first, and when she waved me on, I answered Agatha. "Well, we were going to discuss that tonight. We've talked about several things—the Dixie National Forest sounds beautiful, Salt Lake City, and maybe even Park City or somewhere farther north."

For some reason, I suddenly remembered something. I shifted my focus over to the guys at the far end. "Hey, Eugene … I was supposed to deliver a message: 'pass the salt'." I saw instantly that I probably should have kept my mouth shut.

Without warning, Eugene stood up, grabbed his chair, and motioned for Agatha to do the same. Shadow leaped up and started barking.

"What?" I laughed hesitantly. "Where are you going? What does that even mean, Eugene?" My heart skipped a beat and I felt my face flush. *What did I do?*

He turned to me; his normally bright eyes cast a very dark menacing look. "Stay out of my business, Libby!" Shadow barked again and started to follow Eugene. Agatha shot me a look of apology.

"Shadow! Get back here…" I shouted. "Really, c'mon Eugene, tell me…" He just kept walking.

Agatha shrugged her shoulders at Alexis and me, but followed her husband to their truck. The doors slammed, the engine roared, and off they went.

JJ looked my way like a wounded animal. "What? Why ... *why* did you do that? We were having a great conversation," he pouted.

"Do *what*?" My mouth hung wide open as I watched JJ walk away too. I looked to Lexi, "I don't understand."

"Sweetie, what was it you told Eugene?" she asked.

"Pass the salt."

She thought for a second, then shook her head, "I have no idea. Where did you come up with that?"

"The girl in the bathroom..." I didn't know what was happening so I just stood there shaking my head dumbfounded. Greg came over and put his arms around me.

"It's okay. We need to call it an early night anyway," he said.

Lexi came over and gave me a tight hug. "Don't worry, Libs. JJ will get over it ... I'm sure he was just enjoying the conversation with Eugene. I'll go see if I can learn more. You guys get a good night's sleep," she said, and then walked away to their camp.

I clipped Shadow's leash on and we took her for a walk around the lake. I needed to clear my head. My body was exhausted from the hike, but needed movement after sitting for hours. My brain was buzzing while trying to comprehend what I'd done. And, mostly, I was so sad that I had ruined a perfectly good evening with friends ... and I didn't even understand fully how, or more importantly, *why*.

We walked along in silence and let Shadow sniff all around. There were two other camps that we passed. They seemed to have packed it in for the night because we didn't see any people out. As we made our way back to our site, I noticed a vehicle on the upper road, the main one you take before you turn into the campground. There was something familiar about the truck, but I couldn't place it. It was pulled off to the side of the road.

We gathered up several bottles and bits of trash around camp before we opened the door and went inside. I unleashed Shadow and patted her butt, encouraging her to take the steps inside. She must have been as tired as the rest of us—it took a second before she got the umph to hop up. Once she was inside, I turned around to make sure we picked up everything. I looked back up toward the main road. There was someone standing with the driver's door open, presumably looking our direction, but it was dark enough that I couldn't see details. The person had a ball cap on. Then, it hit me. Blue, lifted truck … it was the one that peeled out of the parking lot at Ruby's!

We *were* being followed.

CHAPTER NINETEEN

I've tried calling her phone several times," I explained to Greg. "They're not answering."

"Let's just settle in. We'll catch up with them tomorrow and find out more. I agree, the message you passed along seemed benign. And, you are just the messenger. But, there's nothing we can do about that now. Want some popcorn?" He flashed his gorgeous smile and moved to put his arms around me.

"Popcorn sounds great!" I went to change into my warm fleece lounging pants.

Greg put the package into the microwave and a couple minutes later the smell of buttered popcorn was overwhelming. I plopped down on the cushy sofa and accepted the small bowl Greg handed to me. Shadow curled up on the floor just below me. She wasn't dumb—

this is exactly where I was bound to drop pieces of our snack.

"That blue truck was just hanging out up there on the road?" Greg asked, before he sat with me on the couch. He had his own bowl of popcorn, which made me realize what I adore about him—he's a smart man.

Smiling to myself, and then realizing he'd asked me a question about the truck, I looked up. "Yeah. It sure looked that way. And, I'm sure it's the same one I saw in Bryce yesterday. It's unmistakable—that color blue is like a robin's egg. You just don't see many trucks that color. And, it's *huge*." I lifted one arm indicating a very tall truck. "If it belongs to that girl from the bathroom, it's strange because it looked like a guy standing next to it tonight. Maybe there's two of them? Maybe she doesn't own the truck? Maybe he was the getaway driver after her little display in the restroom?"

"I just don't care for the possibility that you were specifically targeted at those restaurants. And then, a similar truck is seen near where we are staying—which is miles away from either of those locations. Definitely means we've been followed."

"Hey, early in the morning, let's take a drive around town and just see if we find that truck parked outside a home. Maybe if we were able to get a license plate or, even better, a home address, JJ could help us identify who it belongs to?"

"That's a good idea."

With a plan now in place, I felt like I could relax more. We enjoyed our popcorn and a movie before falling asleep just before eleven.

* * *

It was five o'clock when I first stirred. Once I opened my eyes, I realized why I woke. Greg was already up and brewing the coffee, and the aroma was finding its way to the bedroom. I stretched and then got out of bed. As soon as my feet hit the floor, Shadow jumped up and wiggled around, very excited for a whole new day. I hurried to get dressed and put some shoes on.

"Good morning!" I said, coming out of the bedroom. Near the front door, I reached for my jacket and Shadow's leash.

"Coffee is almost ready, sweetie. Did you sleep well?" he asked.

"So good. Better get this pup outside before it's too late…" I opened the door and Shadow leapt out, nearly pulling me with her.

We took a nice long walk near the lake, enjoying the twilight of the cool morning. There were ducks on the water, bunnies running around everywhere, and I could hear coyotes howling in the distance. I took several deep breaths and enjoyed the solitude. Everyone would be up soon and then we'd have constant activity for the rest of the day. For now, I savored the time lost in my own thoughts.

Of course, my thoughts went directly to Eugene and Agatha. We knew that he was after his former wife's family's valuables, which had been hidden throughout… well, hmmm, throughout *where*? The Southwest? Isn't that what was written on the piece of paper that I found in their camper? The Southwest is an awfully large area. And, if that was a clue where to find the treasures, why did they spend so many years in places like the Midwest? Didn't Agatha mention Pennsylvania and some locations back East? What led them there?

What were the other 'clues', if that's even what they were? Something about the sea ... and, fish? Okay, strange. What do any of those things have to do with the desert in Utah? Shadow lurched toward a bunny that ran in front of us, and that brought me back to the present. I jerked the leash, "Leave it, Shadow." I said sternly.

We climbed the steps back at the RV and when we were inside, I saw that Greg was dressed and the insulated to-go coffee mugs were filled. He was ready to go.

"Should we take Shadow or leave her here?" I asked.

"I'm sure she'd love to go for a Jeep ride." He smiled and kissed the top of my head.

We gathered our stuff and then quietly loaded it into the Jeep, trying to be respectful of the other campers who were still asleep.

Panguitch was around fifteen miles from the lake resort where we were staying, and was not a large town by any stretch. I think I read that the population was less than 1,700. The whole town was only about three miles long. As we drove down the main drag, I got caught up in the old-time feel of the small community. The buildings, mostly brick, reminded me of a quaint old western-style town. It was cute. There weren't many people out at this hour; the sun had risen, but it was still only around six-thirty in the morning. So far, no sign of the robin egg blue vehicle we were looking for.

We started at the far end of town and drove down each

city block on either side of Main Street as we made our way through. The houses varied from worn-down and greatly in need of a paint job, to gorgeous brick or wood homes that were tended to with love. The farther away we got from Main Street and on the outskirts of town, there were more log cabin style homes on acreage. If I were wanting to settle in a small town, this very well could be the one. I smiled to myself thinking about what a nice, quiet life it would be here.

"I haven't seen anything resembling the truck you described. You haven't said a word, so I take it you haven't either?" Greg asked.

"Nope, nothing."

We ventured back through the center of town, where we both spied a donut shop to our right. Without words, our shared glance said it all—we pulled in.

"I hope they have chocolate sprinkle raised donuts!" I was already salivating as we walked up to the door.

"Fairly specific, I'd say," Greg teased, then grinned. "I'm hoping for a maple long john." He held the door open for me, and that's when we saw Todd.

I walked straight over to his table.

"Hey, how are you doing?" I looked down and saw his leg encased in a large black compression boot, propped up on a chair.

He glared. "Not working, that's what!"

Greg had caught up to me just in time to hear the callous response.

Todd continued, "If it weren't for your damn dog, I wouldn't have fractured my ankle! I'm going to sue you!"

"Now, wait a second, Todd," Greg calmly tried to quiet the man down. "It clearly was an accident. The fairly deep sand, you were running, it's easy to twist..."

"Shut up!" he yelled.

I grabbed Greg's arm, gently suggesting that we go order our donuts and get out of here.

The girl at the counter seemed sympathetic, almost as though she'd already sustained the wrath of Todd. She patiently packed up a dozen-sized box with a variety of donuts. I ordered a couple hazelnut lattes for myself and Alexis. Greg and JJ were easy—they preferred the coffee we brewed ourselves and there was plenty of that back at the trailer.

Before we left, I turned back toward Todd. Greg hesitated, shaking his head at me, knowing it was a bad idea to continue down this path.

"Todd, we're just trying to help Eugene. You ran from us that day—" I started.

"Eugene needs to find my family's valuables, like *now*. I'm in deep and I'm tired of his farting around." He huffed, moved his leg from the chair, and tried to stand. After a couple wobbly moments, he got his balance and towered over me. "Where is the old man?"

"Listen. Help us help you. We can all work together and find what you need."

His head tilted to the left. He didn't immediately start yelling so I thought we were making progress, finally.

I tried to press further. "You say you're in deep. With who?"

"I don't have to tell you diddly ... now, go tell Eugene we're finding the rest of the stuff *to- day*!" he said the last part with clinched teeth, then hobbled out as best he could with his walking boot.

Greg held the door open for the injured guy, then we

both walked out to hear Shadow barking like crazy from the Jeep. She was full-on alert screaming, looking pointedly at Todd. We both watched as he rounded the building, going out of sight. As we calmed Shadow down and got loaded into our car, we heard the diesel engine.

"Look! There goes the blue truck…" I yelled. "Follow him."

Greg quickly snapped his seatbelt in place, started the Jeep, and slammed it into Reverse. We squealed the tires on the asphalt when he abruptly punched the gas in Drive, heading out to Main Street. The truck sped through town and was now about a quarter mile ahead of us, but it didn't take long to catch up.

Todd pulled off on the road that would take us to the lake. We held back a little bit since there was no traffic around. Not long down the road, he made a left turn onto a dirt road; we followed the cloud of dust at a distance. He turned left again. We saw that he pulled into a driveway of a small log cabin-style home. We decided not to make the turn since we could see the house from where we were. A smaller, chunkier guy with a baseball hat, baggy jeans, white T-shirt, and a loose green jacket quickly climbed up into the truck. We moved on down the road in case they came right back toward us. We pulled off into a driveway of a home that appeared to be deserted. As soon as we saw the two pull out, we waited for a moment and then followed.

They turned onto the lake access road.

"Suppose they are headed to our camp at the lake, looking for us…" Greg started, "or, Eugene?"

"Does this road lead anywhere else besides the lake?" I wondered.

"Oh, yeah … 143 goes on to Cedar Breaks National Monument. I think you can also go that way to Brian Head. The ski resort."

"Then, maybe we're being paranoid."

We kept following and sure enough, they went on past the campground turnoff.

"Thank goodness. You know, let's just leave it. He's unstable and I'd rather eat donuts right now." I smiled at him, and Greg agreed. We turned around and headed back to the campsite.

"I'm proud of you, Libby. Didn't think you had it in you," he grinned broadly.

"What?"

"*You* turning away from a *mystery*…?" He laughed and I just shrugged as I opened the donut box and pulled out my chocolate with sprinkles.

CHAPTER TWENTY

Our friends were sitting out, enjoying the morning view of the lake when we arrived.

"You early birds must have got the worm," JJ laughed.

"No worms, but I've got donuts!" I cheered, holding the box up as I approached. Greg followed, holding our lattes.

"Hazelnut?" Alexis asked.

"You bet!" Greg handed her the hot cup of coffee and I sat down next to her.

"You've been gone awhile. I heard when you pulled out." Alexis was inquisitive.

Greg piped up, "We just wanted to scout out the town a little more. Figured we'd find a bakery or donut shop— and we did!" He glanced over to me and I understood we shouldn't say anything further about Todd.

JJ grabbed one of the chocolate long johns. "Did you ever reach Agatha or Eugene?"

I shook my head and picked at crumbs I'd dropped in my lap. By the look on her face, Shadow was disappointed they hadn't fallen all the way to the floor.

"Where were they staying?" Alexis asked.

"I think it was the Lamplighter?" Greg said, then looked to me. "We could have checked that out, we drove right by there."

"It was still so early though."

We sat around enjoying the morning, and decided that none of us were interested in hiking today. All of our muscles were screaming at us, and we all agreed an easier schedule today was in order. We bantered back and forth on ideas … JJ wanted to go fishing again in this lake; I wanted to take a drive somewhere; Alexis wanted to read; and Greg was good with any one of those ideas. In the end, we decided to take a drive to find Eugene and Agatha at their hotel before it got much later. Then, we'd see about renting a fishing boat for the day. JJ, Greg, and I would go fishing while we left Alexis on her own to enjoy a nice quiet book.

When we pulled up at the Lamplighter, we didn't see their truck and boat in the parking lot. The clerk at the front desk told us they'd checked out earlier. Greg remembered the garage where their RV was being repaired, so we swung by there. It had been finished and the duo already took off. The repairman didn't know, or didn't want to tell us, where they were headed.

"Well, that's that. But, knowing them … we're bound to run into them again soon," Alexis said.

I wasn't so sure. Eugene was quite upset at me last night.

"Let's head over to that rental place and get us a boat!"
JJ was excited to get out on the lake.

* * *

My phone rang and it startled me, as we sat quietly in
the middle of the lake, waiting for a fish to bite.

"Agatha!" I exclaimed.

"Gotta make it quick," she whispered. "Just wanted
you to know that we left this morning. I feel bad for how
it ended last night. I don't know what was wrong with
Eugene."

"He didn't say why I upset him?" I asked.

"Not a word. But, he was adamant this morning that
we pick up the RV and get an early start."

"Are you in Cedar City?"

"No." And, then the line went dead.

I quickly sent a text: **Are you okay?**

Greg pulled in his line. "So, how are they doing?"

Sitting there for a second in silence, I slowly answered.
"I'm not sure. She was whispering. Almost like she was
hiding the fact she was calling me."

JJ looked over his shoulder at me from where he was at
the front of the boat. "That's weird," he said.

"Where are they?"

"*Not* in Cedar City," I said sarcastically. "She hung
up without answering my question." I kept an eye on my
phone in case she texted back. She never did.

We caught a few fish, but no great catch. Once we were
back on land, we all took our turns in the shower house
before joining Alexis with happy hour drinks.

I turned to JJ and Alexis. "What would you guys like to

do tomorrow?"

We had only planned campgrounds through tonight so we needed to formulate tomorrow night's destination. Originally, we had thought we'd head through the Dixie National Forest or potentially head farther north and up to Salt Lake City.

"I'd love to see either Park City or Salt Lake City … heard great things about both of them," JJ answered.

Alexis agreed. "And, if we head to Salt Lake, I'd love to see the temple as well as the lake."

Greg and I had already discussed what interested us. We weren't excited about going into a city as large as Salt Lake City, but we were intrigued about seeing the lake.

"I think I have more interest in Park City—just because it's in the mountains," I added. "But, it's not far from the city so don't see why we can't do both before we turn back toward Arizona?"

We agreed, and JJ went to work getting us reservations.

CHAPTER TWENTY-ONE

Regardless of whether we remained on the scenic Hwy 89 or ventured over to I-15, Google maps was indicating that it would take us around four and a half hours to get to Park City. Taking our time with the RVs and stopping in some cute towns along the scenic route, we allotted six hours for the journey.

Greg turned to me. "Can you check the map again? We're approaching Gunnison and I believe this is where we cut over on Hwy 28 to get to I-15."

"I didn't think we were taking the Interstate." I fumbled for my phone and pulled up the map.

"Yes, but the only way to Park City is to take I-15 for part of the drive. I just can't remember where—this seems too early though."

"Oh, yeah. No, we go farther north and cut over to

Spanish Fork. Still got a ways to go." I smiled.

"Thank you. Glad I've got a good navigator. Might wanna tell JJ and Alexis in case they're having this same conversation." I reached out on the radio and made sure we were all on the same page.

Once we merged onto I-15 just south of Provo, I thought we'd arrived in traffic hell. The speed limit was eighty! And, I swear people were going no less than ninety-five. Tons of semi-trucks, trailers, cars, and huge SUVs … all fighting for the same space. I found myself holding onto the arms of my seat extra tight. I noticed Greg's white knuckles around the steering wheel as well.

"Well, we know the way we *don't* want to come home!" Greg said.

"Not much farther, we're getting off on exit 263 here in a few miles. Hwy 189."

"Good. I need to get away from these crazy drivers." Just as he said it, all traffic was quickly coming to a stop. "Hold on!" he yelled out. He braked aggressively, without locking them up. Everything shook and a couple cabinets came open in the kitchen area. Shadow whined from her place under the dining room table.

Several cars had squealed and turned sideways before making the correction. No one that we could see actually crashed, but we assumed there was a crash ahead of us to have stopped everything all of a sudden. I checked in with Alexis and JJ—they were shaken but okay. The traffic was at a standstill for more than thirty minutes, which gave us time for our blood pressure to come down. I got up and closed the cabinet doors and made sure everything was still secure.

"Definitely, not coming back this way. I hate this freeway!" I told Greg as I was buckling back into my seatbelt. The traffic started to move—very slowly.

"Yep, looks like an RV pulled over ahead … if I'm seeing it correctly. I hope everyone is alright."

All traffic was now being diverted to the far left HOV lane. It took about twenty minutes of crawling along before we saw what had caused the melee. As we passed, my heart sunk. Greg noticed it too. There was a Class-C RV stalled in the right lane and a large tow vehicle was just backing up to it. Over on the shoulder, there was a pickup towing a boat. I saw Agatha standing on the side of the road gesticulating wildly at someone. Eugene was talking to the police.

"Holy shit! It's them …" Greg said. "Should we pull over?"

"I don't think we can pull over two RVs in this mess! We're just going to be in the way. Here, look, exit 263 is another mile away. Let's take it and find somewhere safe to pull over. We'll call Agatha and offer help." I twisted to look back at the scene. "I think the truck and boat are fine. So, I think they still have something to drive and they aren't stranded."

"I can't believe they didn't get wiped out by a semi … or anyone else!"

Our radio chirped and I started talking to Alexis. They were worried about Eugene and Agatha as well, so I told them the plan. As soon as we made it past all the police and could get back in the right lane, it was time to exit. There was what looked to be a college or something, but it had a nice wide open parking lot that we could easily pull into and turn around.

I called Agatha. No answer. That wasn't surprising since they were in the middle of a mess. I texted to let her know that we were only a mile away, and to call me the instant she got the message. All of us had already gotten out of our vehicles and were pacing with worry in the parking lot. My phone rang about five minutes later.

"What are you doing *here*?" she asked immediately. It was difficult to hear Agatha and it was evident that they were still on the side of the highway. "We have a little problem."

"Yes, we saw! We just passed you guys. Are you okay?"

"Oh, we're just fine. The RV was just towed off. Listen, we've gotta get going … the police are done talking to Eugene."

"Ok. Agatha, we are at the very next exit—263!" I yelled, hoping she'd hear. "There's a huge parking lot. You'll see us—come here!" The line went dead so I just hoped she got all that.

Within just a few minutes, we saw a truck towing a boat pull into the parking lot and head in our direction. Agatha looked frazzled as they exited their truck.

"What happened?" JJ asked as he approached with a hug.

Eugene tsked and said, "Oh, that old RV. Gives us fits all the time. I guess they didn't actually fix it yesterday." He was so nonchalant about it.

I went over and gave him a hug. "Are you okay?"

He immediately knew I was asking about more than just the traffic hiccup. He nodded and hugged me back. I felt relief wash over me—we were going to be fine.

It was around one in the afternoon when we decided to find some lunch. There was a Red Robin just up the street, so we unhitched the Jeep and took it, along with the truck, to find food. It was a cool day, so we left Shadow in the RV as our security.

Over lunch, we learned what brought them to Salt Lake City.

"Libby, how did you know to tell me 'pass the salt'?" Eugene asked.

Anxiety started to brew in the pit of my stomach. "Um, remember that restaurant we all went to in Panguitch?" He nodded. I swallowed, then took a deep breath before continuing. "I went to the restroom during dinner. In there was a woman who told me two things." I looked around the table. All eyes were on me. "First, she told me to 'tell the old man he is getting dangerously close.' Second, she said to ask you to 'pass the salt'."

"Why didn't you tell me this that night?" he asked pointedly.

I didn't have a great answer. Why didn't I? "Ummm, I thought she was crazy. I didn't take her seriously."

"Then why did you wait a day and then say 'pass the salt' out of nowhere?"

I just shook my head. "Honestly, I forgot all about her, but there was a moment it came back and then I just blurted it out. I'm sorry. And, I definitely needed to give you more context ... but, in fairness, you just ran off. I didn't get the chance to explain the rest."

He nodded, then took a sip of his iced tea. "No. It's not your fault, Libby."

My heart swelled. I really needed to hear that.

He continued, "Let *me* explain," he looked to Agatha, she nodded and then he continued, "that phrase has been used in my family for years. As a stark warning!"

I gasped. "So, this person knows your family well?"

"That's what I'm afraid of. You see, my mother was

extremely superstitious." He smiled, and took another drink from his glass. "She would *never* take a salt shaker passed to her at the table. You had to set it down first, then she would pick it up. Otherwise, she was convinced it would be very bad luck." Our whole group was intently listening.

I nodded slowly, thinking about what the message actually could mean in this circumstance. It didn't make sense.

"Eugene, do you have any thoughts on who the woman was?"

He just shook his head.

Greg mentioned, "Todd kept bringing up a child of yours. Could she be your daughter?"

"No, I keep telling you guys. I don't have any children. Not from wife number one, two, or three. None!" He was adamant.

I still wasn't putting things together. How would this woman know this about Eugene and his family? Maybe it was a family friend?

Eugene saw that I was still contemplating. "After you told me that, however, I knew we had to get to Salt Lake City," Eugene said quietly. "Now, it makes total sense and I'm glad we headed this direction. Had I also known at the time about the *dangerously close* comment, then I'd have known for sure where we were supposed to head next. I just did it on a hunch. *Salt—Salt Lake City*."

I was confused. My eyebrows pinched together as I formed my question. "But, you just said the salt comment was related to an old superstition? What does *that* have to do with Salt Lake City?" My friends all nodded in support of the question and leaned in for the answer—things just weren't making sense to us.

"Ah! That's the double entendre, isn't it, my dear…" Eugene laughed.

I relaxed a little. "So, you think that not only was it a stark warning, or bad omen, but also a code word for 'go to Salt Lake City'?"

He nodded his head. And, then whispering to make sure he wasn't overheard, he said, "I think she just led me to where I'll *finally* find Evelyn's treasure!" His eyes lit up and he had the childish grin again. Agatha groaned.

It was apparent that there was a lot I could learn from this experienced treasure hunter. It appeared that he knew how to read into *everything*. I just didn't know if I was buying into it at all. Regardless, their adventures sure had added to ours. For the rest of our lunch break, the guys bantered about all the possibilities on where the next metal box would be found. I sat back observing, hoping that we'd still be able to see Park City, but I was afraid we were about to get roped in with Eugene and Agatha again, this time in Salt Lake City.

CHAPTER TWENTY-TWO

I'd never been here before and I was stunned by its beauty. The ski resort town was larger than I'd expected, but I imagined it had grown over the years. With the Sundance Film Festival held here each year, the Hollywood set had certainly found their way to buying property and making this place famous. That, and the Olympics from years back, certainly put Park City on the map.

I was thankful that our group got their fair share of Eugene's tales during our lunch together. Although one part of me really wanted to help find a treasure, I also was torn by wanting to just spend time with my friends and not worry about the elderly couple. As it turned out, we had all decided that Agatha and Eugene were just fine and we left them to go on about their search. We continued north on Hwy 189 and got set up in a campground just southeast of

Park City before setting out to go explore the town.

Once we were actually walking around the center of town, I fully grasped why JJ and Greg wanted us to camp closer to Jordanelle State Park. This place was busy! There was only one RV park that would have been possible for us to pull into easily and it had already been booked up. Instead, the State Park had a beautiful lake, was incredibly scenic and only nine miles down the road.

"Can you imagine this place during ski season?" JJ asked.

"I was thinking the same thing. Hey, let's try this brewhouse…" Greg pointed to a quaint building where people were sitting at tables outside on the sidewalk patio. "Looks like all these places allow dogs." He motioned toward the dog water bowls sitting out. We masked up and followed him onto the patio and took a seat at a table for four.

We enjoyed flights of beer … sampling the various brews, along with some tasty appetizers. All the while, we had the gorgeous backdrop of the ski hills, which were a short walking distance away, and the most fun part was the people watching. The eclectic scene had us guessing *which country* as we picked up on accents from all over the world. Shadow enjoyed the people watching too. Occasionally, she let out a woof, but overall, she was perfectly content lying at our feet and watching the world go by.

"Do you think it was a bad idea to leave Agatha and Eugene on their own in Salt Lake?" I asked the group.

Alexis shook her head. JJ hesitated and said, "I'm not sure we had a choice, honestly."

Greg agreed. "They're extremely independent. They never invited us along or indicated in any way they needed help. So, I agree with JJ, I don't think we had a choice."

"You're right. I keep wavering—going back and forth on being excited; wanting to help them figure out the mysterious hidden valuables, and forgetting all about them and just focusing on enjoying our own vacation."

Alexis laughed. "Libby, you'll never change—nor should you! You *always* want to help people and this is no exception."

JJ interjected, "I just want more time to get Eugene talking about his family history. I *wish* they had invited us along! His story about the salt superstition—so interesting."

"Oh, here we go again—*we could be related…*" Alexis teased, rolling her eyes and laughing loudly.

We all laughed, including JJ.

"Well, I just hope they find what they are looking for. I want them to be safe and I do hope we meet up with them sometime in the future … they are great fun," I said.

Greg shrugged his shoulders. "This trip isn't over yet and one thing that has remained consistent … we keep finding *them*!" We couldn't help but crack up at the truth he spoke. It had been one crazy thing after another ever since we laid eyes on them at Lake Powell. "Who woulda thought? Remember them dancing so lively to that band?"

"And just earlier today … Agatha off on the side of the road!" I laughed so hard remembering her arms flailing around. "You just can't make this stuff up! She is one silly character, I tell you."

Once we were finished eating, we continued to walk through cute shops and see all Park City had to offer. Before we were done there for the evening, we'd signed up for a mountain biking excursion at the ski hills for the next morning.

CHAPTER TWENTY-THREE

Holy…" Greg yelled, stopping short of finishing the expletive just before he took off traversing the steepest hill he'd ever biked before. Hands tight on the grips, braking, then releasing … following our guide all the way down the ski hill.

I was next, then Alexis, followed by JJ and our second guide. We were having the time of our lives. The trails were extensive all throughout the mountain range; we had taken the gondola to the top and then followed the trails for hours. They included some flat trails that linked to steep climbs and then downhill descents of varying magnitudes. Initially, I wasn't completely thrilled on the crazy downhill portions, but eventually, I came to find those the most exhilarating.

We spent all morning on the trails. Our excursion

package included two passes up on the gondola with guides. We were free to use the bikes all day long after the two guided journeys, but once we finished round two, each of us decided we needed a break. Our legs and arms were wobbly when we attempted to stand again. I felt that we were lucky to hobble on into the burger joint at the bottom of the hill—no way I could do another run.

"Wow! That was a blast!" JJ hollered as we walked away from our guides. "I could do that again." I just gave him a look as his legs nearly buckled. He was tired, but just like the man he was, he couldn't admit that.

Greg was still breathing heavily and didn't say much until we were seated with burgers in front of us. "These were well needed," he said, eyeing the burger and taking it to his mouth. "After we're done, are we heading back up?"

Alexis and I were out; we were exhausted. JJ seemed interested.

I looked between each of the guys. "Go back up if you want to; I'm thinking about going back for Shadow and then I wouldn't mind walking her around here for a while. There are a couple stores I'd like to check out that were closed last night."

"Oh, good idea!" Alexis perked up. "I'll go with you. We should take something back for Bella ... and Heather, too."

After eating and resting for a while, it was decided. The guys wanted to play more and we girls were going to walk around town and shop. We'd all meet back here at the burger joint at five.

Strolling in and out of the little specialty shops and clothing stores was not usually my idea of fun. However, today, I was really getting into it. I think it was more about spending time alone with my best friend than anything else, but we were having a great time. The other best part is that this town is so dog friendly. They let Shadow join us everywhere we went.

"Did you see that person who came out of the changing room?" Alexis asked me as she put a skirt back on the rack.

"No, I didn't," I answered as I looked all over the shop. "Why?"

"Oh, I think it was a guy!"

"Maybe it was? I don't think that's as frowned upon as it once was."

"True. Keep forgetting that." Her brows knitted together. "I don't even know why I made it a thing. I'm inclusive of all—of course, it could be a guy in a women's clothing store."

"What do you think about this?" I held up a flowery lightweight summer blouse.

"Mmm, no. Not you." She shook her head and thumbed through the racks. "Maybe like this?" She held up a white blouse with tiny flowers. "It's not as flowery, but still has some…"

"Oh! I do like it better." I held onto it. I have a policy while shopping for clothing. If I find something, I'll walk around with it while looking for more. If I still love it when I'm done and tired of shopping, then I'll try it on. If I love it once I've seen it in a mirror, then I'll buy it. Yes, that's exactly why I don't shop often. It's tedious.

Today I was still holding three items that I loved and wanted to try on. Alexis took Shadow and they walked outside while I tried on clothing. The little flower blouse was super cute—I'd keep. The little black skirt hugged me in all the wrong places—rejected. The blue semi-formal dress was just too fancy—where would I ever wear it;

rejected. With those decisions made, I began the process of getting back into my own clothes.

"You didn't warn him, did you?" A voice startled me. I could see black trainers in the space just below my door.

I hurried to get my clothes back on. "Who's there?"

"He needs to stop the hunt," she said.

"What hunt?" I asked, hoping to keep the black shoes there until I could open the door. "I'm not sure I follow."

With my clothes now on, except for my shoes, I went to yank my dressing room door open. The second I did that, I saw that the feet had moved. I quickly ran into the store. No one nearby. There was a sales associate at the register. Alexis and Shadow were just walking back into the store and saw me looking frantically around.

"Any luck?" she asked.

"Did you see a woman run from the dressing rooms?"

"No. I saw that guy again, but honestly, I've been texting Bella so I wasn't paying attention to who was coming or going from the shop."

"It was the same woman that gave me the ominous warnings in Panguitch ... and Bryce! She just said that I needed to stop him from the hunt ... right in there!" I spun around and pointed to the dressing rooms.

We both walked into the changing room area. All the doors were open and we looked into each one. I also noticed now that the small hallway led to an outer door. I didn't remember hearing anything like a door opening, but perhaps that's where she went. I quickly ran up to the register with Shadow right on my heels. She must have gotten away from Alexis, so I grabbed her leash as I looked up at the girl.

"Do you have cameras at that back door?" I asked her.

She looked at me, bewildered. "Someone just harassed me in the dressing room. I think they ran out the back door. Is there a way to check?"

"There are cameras, but I don't have access to view the footage here. They are all managed at our home office in Salt Lake City. But, that door has an alarm … we would have heard if anyone left that way."

We all walked back to the dressing room and the clerk checked each room plus the back door. Now, right up close, looking at the door, I noticed something peculiar. I leaned closer to the door knob and saw a clear tape poking around the edge of the door. I pulled the door, it easily opened. I poked my head out, but of course too much time had passed and there was no one in the alleyway. Also, no alarm. I turned my attention back to the door; tape was covering the bolting mechanism. I looked to the associate. "Guess that explains why we didn't hear the door latch. But, it doesn't explain why the alarm didn't go off, does it?"

She looked embarrassed. "It has been malfunctioning lately," she said, as she hung her head. "I've told management. I thought it was fixed. Listen, I need to file a report or it'll never get fixed. Can I have you fill out a form about your harassment? What did the person do exactly?"

I agreed to fill out the necessary paperwork, even though I knew it was a complete waste of time and would never amount to anything. The young girl was very sweet and helpful, especially once she realized that they had a security breach. Who knows how many stolen goods exited that door, and for how long? Anyway, that wasn't our issue—I was sure the girl would have a lot more to do, explaining this to her boss and possibly the police. Once we were finished with her, I looked at my watch and couldn't believe how much time had passed.

"We should go meet the guys … it's getting close to the time." Alexis agreed.

We started the half mile walk back to the ski runs. I kept my eyes open for … *who was I looking for?* I had no idea. Someone in a ball cap? Well, that was nearly everyone we passed on the street. Someone in jeans? Well, half the people were wearing jeans—most were wearing shorts because it was a nice day. I didn't have even one valuable detail about the person who kept taunting me when I was most vulnerable.

We found a sidewalk table at the burger place and Shadow helped herself to the community water bowl. We each decided to order a glass of wine. The guys were already overdue, so we assumed they were having fun. We decided to relax and enjoy ourselves too.

"Maybe we should just do something simple for dinner when we get back to the campground? I'm sure the guys are going to be sweaty and exhausted," I suggested.

"We still have salad makings."

"And I believe we have salmon in the refrigerator. We could marinate and grill."

"Sounds like a plan!"

We continued people watching until it was nearly dark. Generally, I'm not an alarmist, but it was getting dark enough that I began to worry. We paid our bill and decided to head over to the bike shop. Just outside the bike hut, we saw the young man who had helped us earlier. I walked right up to him as he was wiping down equipment.

"Hi! Remember us from earlier?"

"Oh yes, hi! You were my first tour today…" he looked confused when he looked down at Shadow. She started to wiggle with excitement. "Oh, hi pup! You are so cute! Hey, where are your husbands?" I decided not to correct him about Greg not being my husband. Not important.

"Well, they went back out on their own this afternoon and we were expecting them back over an hour ago."

"Yeah, they shouldn't be on the mountain this late."

No shit, I couldn't help thinking.

"Can you check to see if their equipment was turned back in? Perhaps we have our signals crossed on where we were supposed to meet up afterwards."

"Sure. Follow me." He led us into the small office where there were a couple laptops set up. "Okay. What was the name on the reservation?"

Alexis and I looked at one another unsure. She said to me, "JJ made the reservations, didn't he?" I shrugged. Then, she faced the young man. "Try Johnson. Jeff, or JJ, Johnson."

His fingers got busy pressing keys on his keyboard. Why does it always seem there are far more keys pressed than the number of characters? Sometimes I wonder whether they fake type to seem busier or more important … or something. Hotels and airlines always seem to come to mind with the hyper-typing.

"Nope. No JJ, or Jeff Johnson listed. Got another one?"

"Greg Lawson," I said, and then waited while he typed for several seconds again.

"Ah, here we go!" His face squinched up as though he was having difficulty seeing his screen. He typed for a few more seconds, then looked at us, "Nope, haven't checked in yet."

My heart sank. Although, I figured if we had the wrong

meeting spot, he would have called by now, I pulled my phone out again just to be sure he hadn't tried. No. My ringer was on full volume and there were no missed calls or texts. Dangit!

Alexis calmly asked, "Ok, what do we do next? It's dark..." we all turned to look out the window and saw only the lights that lit the nearby condos and the walkways along the shopping and restaurant district. "They would be back by now if something wasn't wrong. They could be lost, hurt, or..." She couldn't go there.

"Yep. Gotcha. Let's call the police ... they'll initiate search and rescue." He picked up his cell phone.

I couldn't breathe. This couldn't be happening. Alexis put her arm around me, "Hey, let's not think anything but positive thoughts here. I'm sure there's a good explanation."

I nodded. Swallowing hard, I managed to overcome my sudden dry mouth. "It's just that I'm remembering back to some of those very steep hills. What if..."

She squeezed my hands and looked me in the eyes. "No. We're not going to do that." She folded me into an embrace and I started to cry.

The young man broke through my fog. "Okay, the police are on the way. Do you have pictures of both of them?"

That was a great distraction. We both got busy looking for the best pictures we could find on our phones. As I flipped through all the photos I'd taken over the past week, I smiled. Greg being goofy peeking his head around a tree while hiking at Bryce Canyon; the whole group toasting one night at Panguitch Lake; Agatha in mid-sentence and probably in the midst of telling one of their tales; a contemplative candid shot of Greg sitting with his coffee one morning in the RV … my eyes welled with tears thinking of them alone in the dark somewhere along the forested ski runs.

Alexis giggled. "Look at this one." She showed me her phone screen. JJ and Greg were posing, one arm around one another, just after disembarking the boat we rented at Lake Powell. Their smiles were quintessential JJ and Greg. Beautiful white teeth displaying through joyful, exuberant smiles. I took the phone from her to gain a closer look. My heart beat faster seeing Greg's kind blue eyes. Then I used my fingers to zoom in closer on the photo. There were two people in the background staring at the men. One was tall and thin … long brownish hair. Wait, dreadlocks? That's Todd! Next to him stood someone shorter … not fat, but definitely rotund. It was the same green ballcap. We saw that person get in his vehicle in Panguitch. A chill ran through me as I zoomed back out and confirmed that those two were definitely eyeing our group as we unloaded after the day of skiing.

I decided to not say anything to Alexis or distract from our current situation. I looked up at her with tears still in my eyes. I nodded my head. My voice cracked, "This is the perfect picture of both of them." Tears began to fill her eyes too.

CHAPTER TWENTY-FOUR

Police, Search and Rescue, and many people from the community had gathered in the ski lodge at the base of the hill. The night time cold had set in and there was still no sign of JJ or Greg. The background noise had become the sound of a police helicopter, and multiple ATVs. Occasionally, I could see the large spotlight shining down from the sky and lighting up the forest. Many volunteers were now roaming the ski hills on the motorized vehicles. The sound of two-way radio communications was constant.

I begged an officer to let Shadow and me go with them up the hill. They were insistent that we let the professionals handle it, which did not make me happy. After a few more minutes, a small smile crept onto my face as I accepted the hot coffee that was handed to me by a nice young lady. Alexis and Shadow stepped outside to take a little walk.

Many nice people from the community kept offering us food, but we kept declining. There was no way anything would fare very well in my stomach right now; it was churning and unsettled, as was my worry for this man who'd I'd grown so close to in such a short time. JJ had also been my best friend since our college days, and my heart broke just thinking about the two of them out there in the cold, dark night. However, the only consoling factor was that they were together. Presumably.

A man walked up to me. "Ma'am, this may go on for hours. You and your friend should probably go back to wherever you're staying," the police officer said.

I quickly shook my head, vehemently rejecting what he was saying. "There's no way we're leaving right here," I pointed to the ground, "until they are back here safe and sound!" I had realized I'd yelled all this when suddenly the rest of the room had gone quiet. As I looked around, they quickly went back to their conversations and the police officer just nodded and walked away.

Alexis and Shadow came back into the ski lodge. Shadow ran over to me and jumped up, putting her paws on my lap, and started kissing my face.

"Oh, sweet girl! He'll be back. Any minute…" I looked up at Alexis. "Hear anything of interest out there?" She just shook her head quietly.

"I hung around several people with radios hoping to hear 'we found them!', but it hasn't happened yet." She breathed deeply as she looked around the room. "It *will* happen, Libs. Look at all these people who have gathered in here. Well, there's twice that amount out there on those hills right now. They'll be here soon."

"I can't help but wonder why they haven't called.

They both had phones with them. If they are lost or hurt, certainly one of them would call us. I really want to go search for them myself."

"I know. I've had the same thoughts."

In the wee morning hours, I was growing more weary and more insistent on joining the search. The crowd had diminished, but there was still a constant whir of activity in the background. When my efforts failed to get *anyone* to take me on their ATV, I settled into a quiet corner next to my friend and with my girl curled up at my feet. At some point, I felt myself going in and out of dreams, wondering what was real and what wasn't. I startled, sitting up abruptly, and realized the dream about my father was just that—a dream. It hit me hard then—I could not lose another important man in my life. I just couldn't.

Alexis slowly sat up. "What's going on?"

"Oh, I just had a dream … nightmare really."

"No. Look—over there." She pointed toward the doors. There was a sudden flurry of activity. We jumped up and ran to the doors. Shadow barked and lunged at the door, pushing it open; she ran out and straight for the ski hill. We ran after her.

"Shadow!" As soon as I called her name, I saw where she was headed. There were four ATVs slowly making their way down the bottom half of the ski hill. On the two machines in the lead, there were passengers. Each one had a shiny, metallic blanket over the shoulders. "It's them! Alexis! It's them…" We went running as fast as we could.

The ATVs stopped just shy of the bike rental shack. Shadow was all over Greg as he tried to lift his leg over the seat and to the ground. Once his feet were firmly planted on the ground, he struggled to stand as the driver held out his arm to steady him. Slowly, he stood straight. I ran up and hugged him realizing quickly how unsteady he was.

"Ma'am," said an EMT. "We need to take him over here to be evaluated."

"Are you okay, sweetie?" I said to Greg, ignoring the EMT for the moment.

"I'll be fine. JJ probably needs more attention than I do." He pointed out his friend twenty feet away to the EMT.

I kissed Greg and then let the EMTs take over. I looked to Alexis and she was also struggling to let her husband go. We followed them into the ski patrol's urgent care center.

JJ had a sling wrapped around his left arm and shoulder. They both had bandages on their heads and it was evident they also had many cuts and bruises. Greg kept holding his side and complained of back pain. After the initial assessment of their vitals, the EMTs recommended they be transferred to the hospital for scans.

"We just don't have the proper equipment here to fully assess. He took a pretty good knock to the head," the lead EMT pointed to Greg. Then, he looked to Alexis. "His shoulder needs to be looked at. He could have torn his rotator cuff."

We agreed for them to be transported to the hospital by ambulance. In the meantime, we took Shadow back to the campground and left her in the RV with food and water while we traveled back to the hospital in Park City.

Walking into the lobby of the emergency room brought back so many memories—mostly, of my dad's death, but also of more recent events. Just a few months back, our good friend and client, Sasha, was hospitalized. She was brutally attacked by someone she had met online. At that time, we weren't allowed in the hospital due to COVID-19 and it was heart wrenching to not be there for her. I was thankful now that the restrictions had lessened because I'm not sure what I'd do if I wasn't allowed to be with Greg now. Still, we had to mask up, and thankfully, the hospital had isolated areas for patients with the virus.

We waited in the lobby area while the scans were being done, then the staff showed us into where they were.

Greg looked up at me as I pulled back the curtain in the cordoned off space that he was in. He looked exhausted and like he'd just been in a bar brawl. He had cuts on his face, a large bandage on his head, and several bandages up and down his arms. I couldn't see his legs yet, but since he had been wearing shorts, I was sure they probably got the brunt of it as well.

"I guess we should have just called it a day at lunchtime, huh?" he said quietly.

"What happened, honey? We were so worried!"

"Ugh. What *didn't* happen…" he sighed. "There's a lot that is still blurry," he pointed to his bandaged head. "But, I know that we pushed our limits and probably shouldn't have kept going."

"So, you fell down a mountain? Or…?"

He shrugged. "Again, the details … I hope they come to me. I know that one minute I was gripping the handlebars and enjoying the wind hitting my face. The next thing I knew, I was somersaulting down a mountain, kicking up dirt and rocks. JJ was behind me, but I don't remember seeing him again until we were being helped on to ATVs."

"Oh, jeez … that sounds horrible. Have they said

anything yet about the extent of your injuries? You were complaining about your back when you stood up from the ATV."

"Oh, I'm sore for sure. I don't think it's anything more than that. We'll see."

Alexis poked her head through the curtains. She smiled at Greg. "Hey there—you doin' okay?" He nodded. She looked to me, "Libby, can I see you out here for a minute?" I nodded, bent down to kiss Greg's forehead, and then stepped through the privacy drapes. She took me by the elbow and guided me down the hall, away from our loved ones.

"JJ told me this was no accident. What has Greg said?"

My eyes opened wide. Confused, I tried to recall what he had told me. "Um, Greg ... well, he doesn't remember much. Why, what exactly has JJ told you?" My heart raced; my mouth was dry. "What happened up there?"

CHAPTER TWENTY-FIVE

Someone forced Greg off the trail. There were several bikes that passed JJ, and one of those flew into Greg, sending him sailing." She managed to stay composed while telling me. "JJ was horrified, caught up to Greg and was helping him up. Then he saw the biker off in the distance, just standing in the trees watching them!" She looked around to see if anyone was listening. "Then, JJ took off after him. That's how he got injured. There was more than one—and as he made his way across the trail, another bike shot out of nowhere. The rider had something in his hands, and next thing he knew he was on the ground."

"Whoa! We need to call the police." I was angry all of a sudden. This *was no accident* and I wanted someone arrested. Now!

"Hang on. Let's make sure our men are okay—the

results from the scans should be back shortly. And, yes, we will get the police involved. I'm just not sure if it's going to matter. Do you know how many people do this mountain biking thing?" She was right. How were they ever going to identify the few that were involved? Maybe the guys saw something that could identify them … but already I knew that Greg didn't remember a whole heck of a lot.

Hours later, we learned that Greg had a mild concussion, contusions on his head, arms, legs, and back. There wasn't anything identified on the scans as broken and, internally, everything looked good. However, they told him to take it easy. He'd be very sore for several days and shouldn't do anything too rigorous until the muscles healed.

JJ did have a torn ligament in the shoulder, but thank goodness it wasn't his rotator cuff. He also had contusions; bruising nearly everywhere and same prognosis—he'll be fine, just take it easy for several days and see an orthopedist when he gets back home to make sure the shoulder is healing by then.

With that good news, we checked out of the hospital and headed back to our campground. The rest of the day was spent napping, reading, and taking Advil.

Later that night, we prepared the salad and salmon for dinner. All of us were still exhausted and it'd be an early evening, but I was enormously grateful that all four of us were back together in what had become our 'normal' surroundings. Shadow would not leave Greg's side. She instinctively knew not to jump on him, but she slept curled up right next to him on the bed, or she was on his feet whenever he sat in the chair.

JJ hadn't said much all day. He turned to Greg, "You don't remember that punk kid taking you out?"

Greg shook his head. "How would I? He'd come from behind me, right?"

JJ thought about it. "Yeah, that's right. But, you saw the ones that went after me, didn't you?"

Greg shrugged his shoulders, then said, "I do remember wondering where you were going. You'd just got me seated upright and then you suddenly took off. I remember that."

"There was a dude resting up against a tree ... still on his bike. He was just staring at us. I thought maybe he was the one who caused you to wreck."

Greg's eyes widened. "Oh, right! Then I saw a streak of yellow and bam, you were rolling to the other side of the trail. I couldn't stand up immediately. I'm remembering!"

"Had you had any altercations with anyone earlier? Any idea why these people were seemingly trying to run you off the trail?" I asked.

Both of them shook their heads.

Greg quietly stated, "I remember thinking how quiet the trails had been. Almost like we had the mountain to ourselves. That's what was surprising about suddenly seeing that streak of yellow come out of nowhere and hit you." He looked to JJ for confirmation.

"Yeah, I agree. It had been quiet. What a great time! Well, up until we were injured." He smiled hesitantly.

Alexis had been listening and then touched JJ's arm when she asked, "Where on the mountain were you? Were you on the same trails we took earlier in the day?"

Greg shook his head. "No. No, we went to the far east side. You know where the guide was telling us that there are some great black diamond ski runs? Over in that vicinity ...

way back in the forest. It was so cool!"

She nodded slightly. "Ah, that's what took so long for them to find you then." They both agreed.

"Why didn't you guys call for help?" I asked.

"My phone died," JJ answered.

"Mine flew to who knows where … we never did find it."

I put the finishing touches on our salad and then pulled the salmon from the grill. "Okay, explorers, you're going to need to make your way to the picnic table. Dinner is ready!"

Not long after we were finished with our meal, JJ's phone rang. It was the police. We heard bits and pieces from his side of the conversation, but waited eagerly to learn more. The second he hung up, I asked, "Did they find them?"

"Nah…different police department. It was the Sheriff down in Panguitch. I've got a name and address for the owner of that home you guys followed Todd to. It's a rental, so it's highly probable that the owner—Robert Turner—is not the one you saw that day."

My hope faded and JJ saw it on my face.

"The good news," he continued, "is that we know who owns the truck! Charley Smith."

My optimism found its way back into the broad smile I gave JJ. I knew he could do it. "Okay, so now what?"

"Well, there hasn't been a crime committed so the police really can't pull Charley over until there is probable cause. Or, he commits a moving violation."

"True. And, since it doesn't appear this has anything to do with the woman who has followed me, we're back at square one, aren't we?"

His look said it all.

"Hey y'all, are we leaving tomorrow morning? Or, have we decided to stay here longer?" Alexis asked us collectively.

Greg looked to the rest of us. "We wanted to go to the Salt Lake, right?"

I nodded my head and added, "Maybe the timing is good for that…" I looked at JJ's arm in a sling, "since we need to rest. No more hiking or aggressive activity."

JJ pouted, "I really wanted to go mountain…"

Alexis and I shot him a look that shut him right up.

"Okay, okay. I know." His bottom lip stuck out, but then he smiled. "I don't know what I'm thinking. Honestly, I'm in so much pain, I'm wondering about standing up just to go inside and crawl in bed."

Greg was in agreement with that and made no mention of wanting to do any activity in the coming days.

My phone started to chime and I dug it out of my pocket. It was Agatha.

"Hi there!" I answered, putting it on speaker phone.

"Libby! You guys gotta get here—we *found the treasure!*" The electricity in her voice made our whole group get excited.

"We'll be there tomorrow!" I got the details of where they were camped and we made a plan to meet up at Antelope Island State Park at nine the following morning.

JJ went right to his iPad to make reservations and plan the route. From Park City, we decided to take a more scenic way, avoiding I-15. We'd still be on the Interstate, but taking the northern route would put us closer to the State Park without driving through Salt Lake City traffic.

"How long is the drive? Meaning, how early do we have to get up?" Alexis asked.

JJ pressed a couple more buttons and then used his fingers on the touchscreen to zoom in. Alexis leaned over to see. "We'll go north out of here on I-80, which loops to I-84 and then ultimately puts us right there at the park. It's roughly two hours, and only about twenty minutes longer than going through the city. Which, if we got stuck in traffic again could prove *much* longer."

We all were satisfied with that. Wheels up at seven.

CHAPTER TWENTY-SIX

Eugene and Agatha were both a bundle of excitement once we found them. He hustled us into his RV and had us take our seats. Agatha, Alexis, and I sat at the dining room table. JJ and Greg were across from us sitting on the faux leather sofa. Eugene scooted back to the bedroom area and came back with one of his metal ammunition boxes. We waited eagerly as we watched him open it as though it were a special Christmas morning present. His eyes wide and bright, his face lit up with the same elation that the rest of us were feeling. How exciting!

He delicately pulled out a small leather pouch and carefully poured out its contents onto the dining table. We were transfixed in our spots; us girls sat staring at the table and the guys on the sofa stood silently, moving their gaze from the table to Eugene. We all expected so much more than this—we only saw three gold coins.

"*This* is amazing!" Eugene exclaimed.

I didn't want to burst his bubble, but mine was shattered. "Eugene, tell us about the coins." Maybe there was something I didn't understand, but this didn't appear to be a 'treasure' to me.

He picked up one of the gold coins. "*This* is a Double Eagle!"

The group kept staring intently, hoping for more.

"C'mon, you guys know about the Double Eagle, don't you?" he asked.

We all shook our heads in unison.

"In 1861, there were only two denominations coined—gold and silver. And, only something like eighteen hundred … oh, wait, maybe it's *thousand* … of these made. These were minted in New Orleans! Civil War era…" He continued turning it around in his fingers, eyeing the specific details closely. Then, he handed it over to Greg.

He examined it as closely and we passed it around.

"How much is this worth today?" I asked.

"Oh, probably not much," Eugene answered, as he picked up another coin off the table. "I have no idea."

"And previously you mentioned something about a watch. Did you find that with these coins too?"

He shook his head but never took his eyes off the coin in his hand.

Someone knocked on the door. Quickly, Eugene gathered the three coins and shoved them in his pocket. "Hold on!" he yelled toward the door. He threw the leather pouch in the metal box, put them onto the seat and covered them with a nearby pillow. "Sit closer to that, keep it hidden," he whispered to me as he moved toward the door.

When he opened the door, we could see it was a park ranger. "Good morning!" he bellowed.

Eugene squinted as the sun hit his eyes. "Can I help you?" he asked the park ranger.

"You had asked for information on renting kayaks when you checked in yesterday. Here you go!" He handed Eugene several brochures. "Anything else we can I help you out with?"

"No, not today. Thank you kindly, sir." Eugene was quick to dismiss the gentleman and close the door.

Personally, I didn't understand all the secrecy. From what I'd seen this morning, I wouldn't know this 'treasure' from any other loose coins from someone's spare coin jar. I suppose I was expecting shiny gold bars, and lots of them. Sparkling jewels and stacks of cash maybe. But, three old coins? This treasure hunt wasn't nearly as exciting as what I had going on in my brain.

Eugene's energy quickly turned to action. "Let's go rent some kayaks and play on the salty lake guys!"

Well, that sounded like way more fun than sitting around staring at coins—Alexis and I were all for it. The guys needed to rest and Agatha had no interest; she wanted to stay behind and read quietly.

Our afternoon out on the lake was amazing. Eugene rented a kayak for himself and Alexis and I got a two-seater that we shared. From the rental place, we floated along the shores of Farmington Bay and into little recesses where birds nested and the wildlife was abundant. The contrast of the lake water and the white sand beaches with the distant mountain peaks was stunning.

Eugene was a wealth of information, we learned, as

he told us all about how the antelope had left this area for many years, but were reintroduced in 1993. But, it was the Antelope Island's American Bison population that brought lots of tourists here each year. At least during the great roundup each fall. They were thinking of sticking around for the large festival since it was only scheduled for a few weeks from now.

Once Eugene was done with his history lesson of the area, he veered away from us and took the lead again. We rowed calmly, following him around, and enjoying the peacefulness of the day. Soon, we were back at the pull-out place where we had parked earlier. The kayaks weren't very heavy, but I was impressed how Eugene just pulled his right out.

We left the kayaks exactly where they told us to, then headed into the small country store to settle up our bill so we'd get our deposit back. Eugene headed to the restroom while we girls looked through the snack selection. Apparently, we were hungry because both of us had our hands full headed to the cash register—Bugles, Doritos, Hostess mini-donuts, and Funyuns; things we never eat at home, but which sounded amazing after a day on the lake. I had just set the bag of donuts down when both our heads snapped to our left, trying to locate the source of the commotion.

"Hey! Watch out!" Eugene yelled out. I could see that he was leaned over onto a shelf, where apparently, he knocked several things off and that was the clattering we heard. "Sheesh, what's your hurry?!" He shook his fist.

A woman with long black hair, braided into a ponytail, ran from the store. An employee was right on her heels. Alexis and I left our snacks on the counter and went over to offer Eugene some help. He stood up and smoothed out his shirt, keeping his eyes on the front door where the woman exited.

"I just don't understand why everyone is in such a rush these days! She nearly knocked me over!" He was angry and I didn't disagree. How someone could just push an elderly man out of the way and run off was beyond me.

"Are you hurt?" Alexis asked. He shook his head no.

"We found some snacks we wanted. Anything you'd like to add?" I asked him as we guided him toward the front counter.

"I'd like some beef jerky," he smiled, and then picked out his favorite brand and added it to our pile of junk food.

We loaded up into our Jeep and I drove us back to the campground where we found everyone sitting outside at Agatha and Eugene's site. They were laughing and seemed to be enjoying themselves. We joined in and passed around our snacks.

After we shared the bison history lesson with our guys, Eugene began to get fidgety. He patted his pants pockets, then his shirt pocket. A loud sighed escaped and he got up abruptly and went inside the RV. We'd been watching him, but then went back to conversation. Agatha filled us in on what she was reading; Greg was feeling better, had more energy. JJ was really stiff and didn't like all the pain relievers he was taking.

The RV door swooshed open, hitting the side hard. "Agatha! Where'd you put my coins!!!" Eugene's eyes were wild with fear. "They're not here!"

"I haven't touched them!" she yelled back. "Crazy old bat," she said under her breath.

He stomped back inside and we could hear things

slamming around. Crash! Bang!

"I better get in there and help," she groaned getting up from the lounge chair and set her toothpick on the side table before opening the door. "Stop throwing stuff around—we'll find them. Don't worry!" We could hear her telling him in her gruff voice.

The rest of us sat quietly outside for a few minutes listening to them while they scurried about. Alexis was the first to let the laughter escape. JJ had been holding his in this whole time too. Soon we were all giggling like schoolkids in church. We stopped immediately when their door opened. Eugene stepped out.

"Did you kids see where I put the gold?" he grumped.

We all thought he had put them back into the box, so we replayed everything that happened since we first learned of the coins earlier in the morning. Step by step, we walked through the reveal all the way to the point where the park ranger knocked on the door.

"OH!" Alexis shouted out. "You shoved them into your pocket when the knock at the door happened!" She was very proud of herself, just as one would be if they won a game show contest.

I remembered that, too. "Yes, Eugene, remember when you shoved the box under the pillows and told me to hide it? Right before that, you put the coins in your pants pockets." He was patting himself down again and it was evident, they were no longer there. The expression he had was of pure sadness and I felt for the man.

"Okay. So, we know that's where they were at that point in the day. Let's review everything we've done since then," Greg suggested.

We left for the kayak rental place soon after the park

ranger left. That was probably how he forgot to put them back safely in the ammunition box—he was so excited to get out on the lake. *Oh geez, did they fall in the lake?*

"That woman!" he hollered. "The one that bumped into me in the store. She pick-pocketed me!"

We all looked at one another—*that* was a possibility. And, much easier to follow up on than where my mind was going at the bottom of the lake.

Eugene, Greg, and I hopped into the Jeep and off we went.

CHAPTER TWENTY-SEVEN

The manager at the general store where we rented the kayaks was very helpful. He informed us that the employee had caught up to the woman who ran from the store, but we were gone by that time. They interviewed her and she willingly emptied her pockets and showed them she hadn't stolen anything from the store.

"All she had was some loose change and lint in her shorts' pockets. She hadn't been carrying any bags or a purse. Since we didn't have proof she stole from us, we didn't call the police and we let her go."

"Did she say why she ran away then?" I asked.

"Said she was in a hurry to catch up with her boyfriend. She'd been in the restroom and then panicked when she didn't see him in the store, so she ran out." He turned to Eugene. "She told me she was awfully sorry you nearly fell.

Seemed remorseful enough, I suppose."

"You didn't happen to get her name?" Greg asked.

"You know, let's check at the front desk. She and some guy rented a paddle board. I think she was the only one going out on it, though; he had an injury." We all followed the manager to the front counter. He typed on his keyboard and then looked up at us. "Ok, I just have *Bramm* as a last name … they paid cash—both for the rental and the deposit. Rented it for two hours."

We thanked the man and hurried out of the store.

"Todd followed us here!" Eugene spat the second we were out of earshot. "What does that kid want?"

"And who was the woman with him?" I wondered.

"I don't care what she told this guy," Eugene pointed to the store, "*she* pickpocketed me! I'm even more sure now, learning that Todd's involved."

We both looked at him like he'd sprouted horns.

"Okay, okay … Todd is hunting us down again, I get it!" Greg held his hands up in surrender. "Just strange that he'd give his real last name if he's going incognito."

That was a good observation, but I wasn't ready to give Todd any intelligence points myself. More curious to me— who was this woman with him? Had he dumped the earlier guy that we saw him with? We headed back to the Jeep, but just before climbing inside, I asked them to wait for me while I ran back inside.

I saw the manager still standing at the register. I waited my turn while he checked out a man in front of me.

"How can help you?" he asked when I approached the counter. "Did you guys remember something else?

I nodded. "When you were questioning that woman, the one you thought was shoplifting, did you learn where she was staying?"

"Actually, I got the impression she was staying here at the campground. What did she say…" he contemplated for a second, "for some reason, I think it was White Rock. What campground are y'all in?"

"We're at Ladyfinger."

"Ah, okay," he pulled out a map. "See right here's where you are … and, over there," he pointed to the top of the island, then moved his finger south, "is where I think they're staying."

"That's very helpful. Thank you!"

"Now, don't go causing any trouble—she didn't mean your grandpa no harm!" he yelled after me as I was already through the door.

I hurried over to the Jeep and crawled in, feeling very proud of myself. "Let's go check out the other campgrounds, I think I might know where they went."

Greg drove slowly through White Rock Bay Campground and Eugene and I looked carefully at each camp. I was looking for a lifted blue truck and Eugene was looking for the woman who plowed into him. I just had a hunch that we'd see the truck here. It seemed to be wherever Todd is, so I thought it was a safe bet.

He rounded the corner and we drove down the next row of camps. The park was not very large so it didn't take long before we were back at the entrance. No blue truck. No familiar woman.

"Well, let's try Bridger Bay before we make it back to ours?" I suggested.

Greg nodded. "Might as well."

After doing a similar jaunt through the next camping area, we struck out and headed back to the rest of the group. I was disappointed, but honestly, I didn't think it was really going to be that easy to begin with. And, what were we going to do—ask for the coins back? And when they denied having them, then what? All this felt very defeating. I felt bad for Eugene. I know he had to feel stupid for leaving them in his pocket and not securing them back in the box. Also, I considered, what if they fell out somewhere along the way—the lake while we launched the kayak, the bathroom when he used it, or anywhere along the way. It was possible that he lost them and they weren't actually stolen.

"Eugene—do you have any other ideas where the rest of Evelyn's family valuables may be?"

"I have one more clue—Big Fish," he sighed. "That could be *anywhere*."

Yes, it could. We'd already been to many lakes in the southwest region and we hadn't even touched the surface with how many there were left to explore.

We arrived back at the camp and dropped Eugene off at his trailer. We were at the other end of the campground, so we drove around the loop and pulled up to find Alexis and JJ grilling some hot dogs. Shadow was at their feet hoping something would fall.

"Any luck?" Alexis asked, as we walked up to them. Shadow ran over and jumped up for a hug. I gave her love and then she soaked some up from Greg as well.

"Not really." I told her the story the manager had given us. "Do we have chili for those dogs?" I asked.

JJ pointed to the pot he was stirring with his good hand, "Right here. You and I are thinking along the same lines! We've already got the onions diced and cheese grated, too." He flashed a smile.

"Better get cleaned up then," I said. Greg opened our

trailer and we climbed in.

During dinner we plotted our next steps. "How are you guys feeling this evening?" I asked.

Greg was still feeling pretty good. JJ grimaced, which told me the pain hadn't subsided. "Would you rather stay put for a couple more days, or journey on, slowly heading south to make it back home?" I asked.

They both looked at each other. Greg left it to JJ.

"I really don't want to drive long distances. My shoulder needs rest—if it were a car I was driving, that would be one thing, but the RV requires a bit more effort to keep it on the road." We all agreed with that and sympathized with our friend.

"Okay! Then, let's just get comfortable here for a little bit. Maybe we can continue helping Eugene find his coins and then in a couple days, we'll head for home." I filled them in on my thoughts earlier that Eugene could have lost the coins anywhere.

CHAPTER TWENTY-EIGHT

The next morning, Alexis and I headed back to the State Park rental store. It was a new crew working; we didn't see the manager that we'd spoken to yesterday. That's not why we were there though. We decided to rent electric bikes and scout out the island. We left Shadow with the guys, who were resting. They were thinking about floating in the salty water later. We decided that would be a perfect activity for a boisterous puppy to do too.

I'd never ridden an electric bike before so we got schooled on the features before we set off, following the State Park map. There were trails just for hiking and then multi-use paths for bikers and hikers. Hikers had the right of way. Once we got in a rhythm, both of us were smiling and having fun. Mainly the terrain was level, but occasionally, we came upon a spot where just a little pedal-assist really helped. I could get used to this!

We followed a trail all the way down to Fielding Garr Ranch and then made the loop north and diverted to our left, following another trail. There were very few hikers we had to yield to, so we just kept going. One thing we probably should have been told was that after a couple hours, we should be close to our ending point or the batteries would die. We figured that out with several miles to get back. Yes, we could pedal, but that was also the point in time where we were tiring out.

Alexis pulled off the trail in a wide spot in the dirt. "Look over there. How cool would that be?" She pointed out where there were four tent campsites right next to the water.

"I'd *love* that … let's ride over there!"

We pedaled around the trail loop where it led us into that camping area. Two of the sites were taken, and that's when I stopped dead in my tracks. I saw the truck parked at the end of the path—about twenty yards away.

"Lexi, that's the truck I've been looking for!"

Her eyes got huge. "You think those are the people following us?"

I nodded my head slowly and decided to pedal over there. "Shh, don't call attention to us. Let's just nonchalantly ride by." She didn't look convinced we should be doing it, but she followed anyway.

It was definitely the truck I'd seen before. There were two muddy mountain bikes hanging over the tailgate. A dark-orange tent filled the small site, and there were several lines strung between trees where clothes were drying. Looked like several camouflage patterned shirts and shorts, tan hiking pants, a yellow jacket, and numerous pair of underwear. I'd say they were all men's briefs; I wasn't seeing evidence of a woman in camp—at least based on the hanging clothes, anyway. I also didn't detect anyone around, unless they were sound asleep in the tent. We moved on past their site and stopped back at the entrance to the tent camping area.

I pulled out my phone, taking a picture of the whole area. Then I zoomed in on the blue truck and snapped another, which I sent in a text to JJ. **Look who we found? There's a tent-only camping area on the island—looks cool!**

Pedaling out of this area was on a slight incline—one that would have been great to use the pedal assist feature had our batteries still been charged. We huffed and puffed the mile or so to the main road and coasted until we came to another wildlife loop trail. Alexis stopped and I pulled up next to her.

"Wanna continue, or is it time to head back since our batteries have died?" she asked.

"I'm game if you are. I'm enjoying pedaling. Well, not up that last incline…" I smiled pointing behind me.

"Okay! Let's go!" She led the way.

The birds were plentiful and we actually saw antelope in the distance. It felt like we were the only ones out today and we were thoroughly enjoying ourselves. I was having visions of running into bison, which would definitely ruin our day. I was fairly sure they weren't roaming in this area, but at the same time, how would I know that? I kept looking behind me with that feeling of being followed … by a monstrous brown hairy beast with horns.

What I came to realize very quickly is that I should never look behind while riding. By the time I looked forward, it was way too late—I had already slammed right into a huge yellow beast instead. My foot caught on one pedal as the rest of my body dragged the ground. I rolled several feet, landing in a white sandy marsh filled with cattails, feeling the cold moisture seeping into my pants. I spat out salty, gritty debris from my mouth. My helmet was askew. As I straightened it and looked skyward—daylight was stolen from me. Everything went dark.

CHAPTER TWENTY-NINE

"Oh look, I got a text from Libby earlier!" JJ announced. He, Greg, Eugene, and Agatha were sitting around Greg's camp wondering when the girls would be back. They'd been gone most of the day, and since daylight was diminishing, they expected to see them pull up in the Jeep at any moment. "It's a picture of a truck and she says the tent-only camping sites look cool."

Greg turned toward his friend. "No mention of when they'll be back?"

"Nope. But, look at this picture…" JJ handed the phone over.

"That's *the* blue truck, isn't it?" Greg felt a nervous swell in his gut. "The one she had you research the plates on?"

JJ took the phone back. "Oh, yeah. I see that now." He

looked to Greg again with wide eyes. "So, they *are* staying here."

Neither of the men were comfortable knowing their partners weren't back yet *and* had apparently come across the person who had been following them around Utah.

"When did that text come through; how long ago?" Greg was hoping it had been within the last few minutes, but all hopes were dashed when JJ told him it was several hours before.

Eugene had been following their exchange carefully. "Do you think you know where that pickpocketer is?" They both nodded. "Well, let's go get her!" The spritely old man was up and headed to his campsite before anyone could say a thing. He drove up to them in the truck, "C'mon let's go!"

"Okay. Guess we're going." Greg, Shadow, and JJ loaded up into the truck, leaving Agatha at the camp. JJ stuck his head out the rear window, "Agatha, text me if they get back here while we're gone."

"I don't have your number!" Agatha hollered after the truck as it pulled away.

Using the Antelope Island map they'd picked up earlier in the general store, JJ was navigating them to the 'tent-only' campsites. They pulled off onto the side road that led them toward the water. Slowly, they passed each site—there was only one occupied. It looked like there was a young couple lighting their grill. They stopped.

"Hi! Excuse me…" Eugene called to them. The young man wandered over. Shadow barked at him.

"Good evening, what can I do for you? Oh, what a gorgeous Lab!" Shadow was now on JJ's lap, leaning out the window licking the man.

"We're looking for our friends. Two ladies—both

would have been on those new fangled bikes." Eugene struggled to find the words to describe so Greg helped.

"They rented the electric bikes and we know they came through here. Have you seen them? One white female, has auburn hair—probably pulled into a ponytail. She's about five-foot-six 'ish. Her friend is slightly taller—five-foot-eight, dark skin, short cropped hair. Oh, of course, they had helmets ... shoot, JJ what color were their helmets?"

JJ thought for a moment, "They were rentals and we weren't there when they got them. But, remember when we saw those other people returning their rented gear yesterday—they all were a similar black with silver reflective stripes. Isn't that right?" Greg nodded in agreement.

The young man thought for a few seconds. "We just got back here ourselves not that long ago. Been out on the lake all day. I'm sorry, I don't recall seeing them." His companion walked up just as he finished, completely enthralled with the dog her partner was petting. "You don't remember seeing bicyclist through here, do you?"

She took over the Lab petting job, "What a precious ... girl?" she asked JJ. He nodded. Then she recalled something. "Oh, remember when we were floating over there by the marshland area ... the bird preserve? We saw a couple bicyclists going by then. Must be a trail over there? Haven't been down it yet."

"Oh yeah, we were so far away though. I couldn't tell you whether they were the ones you've described to us," he turned, saying collectively to the car full of men.

JJ struggled to get Shadow back to her side, then grabbed for his phone. He reached out the window and showed the guy the picture Libby had sent. "Do you recognize this?"

The girl immediately answered, "Oh sure! They were

camped just over there." She pointed to a site not fifteen yards away. "Looks like they packed up and left today though. A guy and his friend—very nice; they came and shared a beer with us last night!" she said proudly of their newfound friends.

"Did they tell you their names?" Greg asked.

The two looked to each other, then he answered, "The one with long hair was Todd. Um, the other one … seemed like a guy's name. What was it? She was the one who was very, uh, well, I guess…*masculine*. What was her name?"

"Charley!" Just like she won a contest for a valuable prize, the young woman jumped and clapped as she remembered.

"That's right. Charley and Todd. Those were their names."

"And they said they're leaving today? Did they say where they were going next?"

The excited contest winner, spoke rapidly, "Uh, yeah, that's what's weird … Todd said they were staying several days. They were having so much fun—kayaking, bicycling—you know, they had these amazing mountain bikes…"

JJ cut her off. "Ok, so they hadn't planned on leaving. Do you find it odd that their stuff is gone now?"

"Yeah, man. I was surprised when we rowed up to shore and they were already gone." The young guy answered as he fidgeted, putting his hands in his pockets.

Eugene asked, "Is there anything else you can think of?"

"Why are you looking for those two? Did they know your friends?"

"That's what we're trying to figure out," JJ answered.

"You've been a lot of help, thanks!" They waved goodbye and slowly pulled over to the empty campsite.

Eugene put the truck in Park. "Let's take a look around."

Shadow quickly agreed and leaped out over JJ as soon as he'd opened the door. The three got out also and started carefully scoping the area. At first glance, it looked spotless. Shadow was sniffing all around, heading right over to the water's edge. JJ pulled out the picture again where they could see that along with the tent, there was a table, grill, camp stove, several clothes lines, the truck, along with mountain bikes. It was a considerable amount of stuff to be packed up.

JJ was reading off his phone. "The picture came through as a text at 3 p.m. It's now 6:10 p.m. Plenty of time for someone to pack up camp and leave. Question is: why? If they told their fellow campers they'd planned to stay in the area for several days, what exactly prompted them to leave?"

"Do you think Libby and Alexis confronted them about Eugene?" Greg asked with a sinking feeling. "Surely, they wouldn't do that, right? Without us…" Shadow barked and they all saw her sniffing along the shoreline.

JJ didn't answer the question, but looked to Eugene who had been busy scouring the campsite along with Shadow. "See anything of interest?"

"I don't see anything that tells me Libby and Alexis were here, if that's what you're asking. And, it looks like the campers were thorough in their cleanup—pack in, pack out—they did that!"

When they felt there was nothing left to see there, the men corralled Shadow back to the truck and they slowly drove around the loop, back to the main road. Greg was silent as his eyes scanned for any movement in the desert landscape. JJ was casing the other side of the road from where he sat. Eugene crept the truck along as they all expected to see the ladies pedaling through the desert at any point.

Shadow barked with urgency. There was a turnoff for another trail; however, it wasn't meant for motorized vehicles. JJ asked Eugene if he'd pull off on the shoulder of the road to let them out.

"Eugene, you continue driving to the end of this main road … that will put you out near the store. Ask the rental clerk if they've turned in their equipment yet. Then, come back and pick us up here. Got that?" He nodded; Shadow and the men jumped out of the truck. "Oh, do you have a flashlight?" He looked to the darkening sky. Greg clipped a leash on Shadow, soon her black coat would be invisible in the dark of night. Eugene opened the glove compartment, pulled one out, and handed it to JJ through the window. Eugene drove off and the friends headed down the trail.

At the beginning of the trail, just as they passed the fence line, Shadow whined and sat. JJ pointed, "Look here. A vehicle pulled out from here—see the tire marks. Looks like it had been backed right up to the trailhead maybe."

"Yeah, I see that, but anyone could pull off the road— like Eugene did—and get turned around." Shadow barked at Greg. "What, you don't agree?" Her tail wagged; she barked again.

JJ smirked at Shadow. "She's a smart dog. Well, let's just keep in mind … here, I'll take a picture of the track marks. You know, just in case."

Before they continued on, JJ consulted the island map again. It showed that the trail looped back to the tent-only campsites eventually. It didn't indicate distance, but didn't appear too far. They kept walking, searching the landscape and trying to hurry along to beat the darkness too. Eventually, JJ turned on the flashlight scanning through bush. Off to the left of the trail, just before it began to loop, Shadow nearly pulled Greg off his feet.

"Whoa! Shadow … hold on!" Then he turned to JJ. "Flashlight, please." He shone light where the pup was trying to pull him. "Look right there." Shadow started barking furiously, pulling Greg. "Shadow. Leave it! Don't worry, we're going to check it out. Sit!" She took her command and sat on her haunches.

"Ugh, it's wet and marshy," JJ's foot had sunk slightly into the wet earth.

He knelt down as he spoke. "No, right there. Tread marks…"

JJ immediately began yelling out, "Alexis!!! Libby!!!" Shadow whined, then made a sound close to a howl.

Greg followed his lead and they continued screaming for the women as they slowly followed the trail alongside the white sand marsh. They heard nothing.

"The trail is heading back to the campsites now … see the fire at the camp we were just at?" Greg pointed. "Not far at all."

Shadow pulled at Greg again, barking.

JJ gasped. "What's that?"

Greg turned back to JJ, "What?" Then he could see something shiny and metallic glistening from one of the bushes next to the road. JJ knelt down and picked up a black helmet with reflective stripes.

Greg nearly threw up.

CHAPTER THIRTY

Eugene had spotted the light from the road he traveled. He followed along on the main road, trying to get close, then found himself back at the one occupied tent campsite. Shadow and the guys were just walking up to it as he put the truck in Park. JJ looked ghost-like. Greg's face spoke volumes—something was very wrong. Then, he saw that Greg was holding a helmet.

The couple had come over to them and offered them drinks. After accepting bottles of water each, the guys shared fearful glances amongst each other. When he spoke, JJ's words indicated he'd now gone into full cop mode. He succinctly stated to Eugene, "We called the park rangers. They are calling the sheriff. We will wait here for them."

Eugene informed them that the rental equipment hadn't been turned in. Greg opened the tailgate on the truck and carefully set the helmet down—it would be evidence now. Shadow put her front paws up on the tailgate and sniffed the helmet intently. She sat back down, right at Greg's feet. The silence that enveloped the small group was only broken by the sounds of the wildlife. It felt like eternity until they finally saw headlights in the distance, but it had only been fifteen minutes.

Greg put Shadow in the truck before the line of vehicles pulled to a stop. One of the officers approached Greg. After Greg explained the series of events that led them to where they were, the officer gave some commands into the radio attached at his shoulder. He informed Greg, "We've already put an APB for the truck plates you gave us." Then, his commanding voice directed toward the rest of the officers on scene, he shouted out tasks. Every person moved into action immediately.

They unloaded an ATV off a truck and two men rode that off toward the trail. Several others headed to the water with their flashlights. Another stayed behind with JJ, Greg, and Eugene, gathering information specific to Libby and Alexis. After another half hour, Greg stood up and walked to the officers who were following the shoreline.

"If it'd help, our black Lab is in the truck. She's really good at tracking scents," he offered. When they both agreed, Greg went back and retrieved Shadow.

On leash, he walked her to greet the officers. She didn't bark at them, but she wiggled and accepted the pets they gave. Then, it was off to work. Greg held onto her leash and gave her lots of rope to sniff around. The group of them found themselves back on the trail. Shadow kept pulling to go faster, and they did. Practically running, they were on a path straight toward where they could see the headlights of the ATV driving away from them.

She stopped abruptly. Her nose went into overdrive, then she bolted from one side of the trail to the other. Greg stood in the middle of the trail giving her all the leash she'd need. The officers shone their flashlights on either side of the trail. Shadow stopped again, right at the heels of an officer who'd hollered, "Over here!" He waded ankle deep into the marsh, reached his hand down and pulled something out of the mud.

It was Alexis' cell phone. There was no mistaking her cover—the jeweled mandala design shone, even through the mud.

Shadow pulled again, this time off to Greg's right. The officer saw it, too. He said, "Look! Something was dragged over here." He followed the indentations in the trail, heading off into the desert bushes. About thirty feet in, behind several large saltbush clusters, there were two bikes tossed aside, hidden out of sight. The officer quickly spoke into his radio and suddenly the ATV headlights were coming back. A flurry of activity ensued. Shadow sniffed the entire surrounding area, but nothing else was found. She and Greg hung their heads as they walked back to the camp defeated.

JJ saw them approach and started walking their direction. "Find anything?"

Greg looked up and said cautiously, "Um, they found Alexis' phone…" he cleared his throat, "and, uh, Shadow found the two bikes." He didn't need to say more. JJ understood that the girls were not with the equipment. They slowly made their way to Eugene who was sitting in the truck. Greg crawled into the passenger seat. JJ passed the truck and went over to the officer in charge to wait.

"I hear that dog of yours was instrumental to my

team." He patted JJ on the back.

"Not my dog, but she is my missing friend's beloved..." JJ got choked up and couldn't continue. He took a sip of his water and sat down on a nearby chair. Through a tight throat, he asked, "Any word on that APB yet?"

"Not yet. They're working on it though."

JJ couldn't imagine a world without his Alexis. What would he tell their five-year-old, Joshua? With his elbows on his knees, he rested his head into the heels of his hands and sobbed.

He wasn't quite sure how much time passed when he realized Greg was standing over him and Shadow started licking his tears.

"Hey, man...we'll find them. Don't worry." Greg looked around at the scene, unsure whether he believed his own words. "They're done tagging everything and it's all loaded in their vehicle now. Let's go back to the camp. Eugene called Agatha hours ago, but she has got to be sick with worry." Greg led JJ by the elbow and they hesitantly left the last known scene of their loved ones.

CHAPTER THIRTY-ONE

Alexis opened one eye, peeking first to make sure their captors weren't around. Her body bounced, hitting her head on something hard. She started to roll and counter-balanced by shifting her hip and thigh over to the left. It was difficult to stay still. *Why?*

She opened both eyes. It was dark but for a slight glow of light. She squinted several times, trying to make sense of her surroundings. It took several seconds, but then she realized she was under a large metal box that was suspended over her. Another bump—she held her bound hands up to prevent another hit to the head.

Sound was now entering her consciousness. *Wind.* Lots of wind. She tried rolling to her right side, but it was too much effort. She closed her eyes again. *Why was it so loud?*

Then, her eyes flew open—*Where's Libby?* Despite the

pain she felt, she rolled to her right. She tried reaching with her right hand, only to have both hands plop onto a bundle next to her. Nothing happened. Her brain registered now—she was lying in the back of a truck. A really *loud* truck.

"Libby!" her voice was barely a whisper.

Nothing.

Then, "LIBBY!" escaped her mouth more urgently.

Another bump. She quickly protected her head again. The bundle next to her shifted when it crashed back down onto the surface they were on. Using her hands, she tried to find an opening on the bundle. She could feel the texture was plastic and crinkled. It was a tarp. Something was wrapped in a tarp. Frantically, she clawed at the covering. Something moved. "Libby!!"

The bundle moaned—at least, she thought she heard something over the loud truck, the wind, and the road noise. It was hard to tell. Then there was movement. She tried again to use her restrained hands to get the covering opened up.

"Libby, are you in there? Do you hear me?"

I could hear a familiar voice and groaned, "Lex…"

"I'm trying sweetie. Are your hands free?"

Alexis couldn't hear my pitiful "Uh-uh." *What was going on?* I tried opening my eyes and wondered if I'd gone blind. It was ink black everywhere. My head was pounding, I felt nauseous, and suddenly claustrophobic. *I've got to get fresh air!* I wrestled my arms up closer to my face and then punched outward. Something shifted, I saw a sliver of light penetrate my tomb.

"Libby! Libby…" Alexis was saying. I felt her body roll over and against mine.

My brain felt like sludge. Nothing made sense. The effort it took to speak or move was exhausting.

"Libby!" The voice faintly broke through the fog. I felt a nudge in my side and tried to open my eyes once again. It wasn't quite as dark. I rolled to my side and moved my arms up to my torso again. After a couple deep breaths, I punched outward again. My arms fell to the hard surface.

"OW!" Alexis yelled out. "Libby…"

I cleared my throat and tried to speak. "Lex…"

"Yes, Libby!! C'mon … I'm right here!"

Alexis was able to use her fingers to move away the hard, cold plastic from my head. I could make out the shape of her head; we were laying face to face now.

"Wh … where … are … we?" I struggled to form the words.

"We're in the back of a pickup. I have no clue how far we've been driven though."

"Greg?"

"Honey, I think we've been kidnapped." Her voice cracked.

"Bikes?"

"Yes! We were biking—I can't remember what all happened, but my body is in so much pain. I think we crashed?"

The vehicle slowed and both of our eyes went wide with fear. We stayed quiet and the road noise lessened. I rolled over onto Alexis as the truck turned a corner and bounced hard onto a dirt road. The road noise increased again, but it was obvious we were at a slower speed than earlier.

"Blue truck?"

"Probably. I have no idea."

I closed my eyes again; they were too heavy to keep open. Alexis kept nudging me, but all I wanted was the darkness to surround me again.

Some time later, my eyes flew open wide. There was no more movement—we were perfectly still. I could hear people talking all around me. *Where's Alexis?* I couldn't see her in her bundle any longer. I just saw metal all around me.

"C'mon, hurry ... someone's going to see us!" a woman's voice sounded urgent, just as someone else grabbed my feet and pulled.

I groaned loudly as my body slid down. Everything hurt—my back, legs, arms, neck. Another set of hands grabbed me around the torso, where the tarp still held most of my body in a tight roll. The covering slid down away from my head and it was the first that I saw daylight. I blinked away the pain for several seconds before I caught sight of a burly looking woman with light brown cropped hair, her face flushed red as she struggled to hold me. She had on a green flannel shirt. I couldn't see the person who was at my feet, but it seemed as though very large hands had hold of my legs. Quickly, I closed my eyes before either one knew I was conscious. I held still.

"Over here ... hurry!" a man's voice sounded.

My body was screaming as they clumsily hefted me for a distance. I prayed they wouldn't drop me, but I remained as still as I could even though I wanted to howl with pain.

"In here. Next to the other one."

The covering started to be stripped off around my body. I kept my eyes closed. They cut through rope, it sounded like, and then my leg splayed out after having been bound for so long. I continued to tell my body to stay limp—*don't move a muscle.*

They must have moved over to work on Alexis' mummy

bag next because I didn't feel them near me any longer. I decided to sneak a peek—gradually looking through a crack in my eyelids. I detected movement a couple of feet away, but couldn't see anyone in my field of vision and I was terrified to move.

"Where are we?" I heard Alexis yell out.

"Shut up!" the man screamed.

Please be quiet, Lex...

"Make sure they're still tied well. Can't risk them getting away now." The woman's voice was familiar—soft in tone, but deep. "Hurry! We gotta get outta here!"

"Okay, okay. I can't move much quicker with this damn foot."

Todd? I wanted to find out if it was really him. I could talk to him—talk some sense... *No, not with her here.* I stayed perfectly still and, thankfully, Alexis did as they asked and quieted down too.

I felt someone move closer to me again. A nudge at my arm. I didn't move. The woman laughed, "Good, this one is still out cold." Then she instructed her partner, "Give that one more chloroform—she needs to go back to sleep for a while."

"Oh, get the redhead's phone ... it's in her back pocket," he demanded. "Ok, this one's out now too—there won't be any sounds from them for a long time."

The woman knelt down next to me and rolled my hip up slightly, reached into my pocket and I felt her slide the phone out. She released me, letting my body jiggle back into place like gelatin in a mold. I could hear more movement all around us, then it sounded as though their foot falls were moving away from us. I risked it and opened my eyes ... just in time to see two shadowed figures pushing a door open, walking through, and then I startled when they slammed the metal door shut. More clanging of metal sounded—*a chain on the door*? I couldn't be sure, but it was dark and we were alone now. I let out all the breath I'd been holding for what seemed like hours.

Attempting to roll to my side, I groaned in pain. My hands were still secured at the wrists and my legs were tied at the ankles. The fogginess that filled my head earlier had gone away and I could see much better as I lifted my hands to my face. The restraints were zip ties.

On my side, I was staring at some machinery and old car parts. We were in a huge metal warehouse style building. No windows that I could see from here. I struggled to roll over the other direction. The pain was searing through my body and I cried out. After several deep breaths, I tried again. Lying on my right side now, my arm was in agony. My hip was too. I opened my eyes after the pain subsided a little and saw Alexis' lifeless form lying on her back, her jaw slack, and mouth wide open. I watched her chest rise and fall. *Good, she's breathing.*

As much as my head was wanting my body to get up and *do something*, I could not move. After what could have been an hour or more, something stirred in me to try and get to a sitting position. I struggled for several minutes, but managed to use my abs and the left side of my body, which didn't hurt nearly as much, and got seated. There was a large toolbox just a few feet away, so I scooted myself to where I could lean my back against it. That had taken all of my energy and I sat there with my head hung, and closed my eyes again. I just sat there listening. Was there anything going on outside that might give me a clue to where we were? I heard nothing.

Alexis started to stir. I became hopeful that if she could also get sitting up, perhaps together we could scoot over to some of the tools across the room and get ourselves out of the zip ties. Of course, it took much longer before her eyes opened and for her to regain consciousness enough to be able to understand me. I just sat there waiting, knowing that every second that ticked by was one second closer to our captors returning.

"Alexis! Wake up!!" I yelled out. "Please … look at me."

She moaned and moved slightly, but her eyes struggled to open.

The light was fading near the creases of the rollup doors and the side door where I saw our kidnappers leave from. It was close to nighttime again. Had we really been here for a full day already?

Alexis opened her eyes and stared at me with confusion written all over her features. It was even darker in the building now, but I could still see her clearly. She blinked away the film coating her eyes. "Libby?" she whispered.

"Yes! Lexi … wake up! We've got to get out of here!"

"Where are we?"

"No idea. But, we're locked in some kind of warehouse and we need to get these…" I lifted my hands, "off so we have any hope of surviving. I don't know when they'll be back."

"Who?"

"Well, one of them was Todd! Don't know who the behemoth woman was though."

Alexis rolled to her side. She laid there for a moment and then pulled her knees in to her chest, hands to the ground in front of her chest, then pushed up into a seated position.

"Wow, that was impressive," I cheered. "It took me far longer to pull off that move."

She gave me a half smile. Then started scooting her way over to me. Once she was near, she also leaned up against the toolbox.

"I imagine the drawers to this thing are on the other side?" She titled her head back at the metal we were leaning against.

I looked around. "Yeah. I wonder how firm this is in place? Think we could use it for leverage and possibly stand?"

We stared at each other for a second and then gave it a test shove with our backs. It didn't budge.

"Ok, one at a time. You go first. Careful," I said.

She pulled her knees in and planted her feet firmly on the concrete. Then, she pushed into the box with her back and used her strong quads to lift herself from the ground. The box never moved at all. Half way up, she grunted, and then gave one hard push to stand.

Breathing heavily, she smiled at me. "C'mon, you can do it too!"

I followed her exact moves and after a couple tries was standing. Alexis hopped to the end of the long metal container, holding on with one hand to keep balanced. She peered around to the other side and saw drawers. "Yes! Certainly, we'll find some tools to get these off." She lifted her arms.

As she opened the first drawer, our heads abruptly turned toward each other. We both heard it. The truck had just pulled up to the building. We stared at each other with fear etched on our faces.

CHAPTER THIRTY-TWO

Greg lay awake, restless most of the night. There was no point in sleeping. Libby was nowhere to be found and his heart hurt. The police said they'd call the moment they found anything. He kept checking his phone for missed calls.

Finally, he got up and brewed some coffee. Shadow looked at him sadly from her place under the dining table. "Wanna go out, girl?" With that, she wagged her tail and crawled out of the space. He put her bra on and attached the leash.

They stepped out into the cold air, and that reminded him to grab his jacket. He reached for it right inside the door, put it on, and slid his cell phone into an inside pocket, and then off they went. Shadow had more pep in her step than Greg did, but they managed to walk a couple miles through the campground before anyone else woke up. The sun was just beginning to peek over the horizon.

Just as they were getting back to their RV, Greg's phone chimed. He reached in his pocket and pulled out the phone to read his text message. From Libby? His heart raced and he found it difficult to get his fingers to work opening the message. Finally, he read:

Help! Bring Eugene—I'm in Panguitch!

He struggled to breathe and his hands were now shaking uncontrollably. He ran as fast as he could to the site next to his and pounded on the door.

"JJ!!!" he screamed. Pounding non-stop. "JJ!! Open!!!!"

He could hear the footsteps running through the small RV and then the mechanisms in the locks turned and the door flew open and JJ was standing there in his tighty whities.

"What, man? Did you find them?"

Greg handed the phone over for JJ to read.

His eyes grew wide and he quickly spoke, "Well, what are we waiting for! Get Eugene and Agatha and let's get out of here!" He handed Greg's phone back and they both got to work.

Eugene and Agatha were already awake and the second Greg told them about the text, they were up and storing their belongings away. All three campers pulled away from the park shortly after nine to make the five-hour drive south back to the small town where they had previously been.

Once they passed through Salt Lake City and away from the bulk of the traffic, he picked up the two-way radio, and buzzed JJ. "Why do you think they were taken to

Panguitch? Seems odd…"

The radio crackled as the button was released. "No idea, man. I just wanna find my wife!" JJ was frantic.

"I hear you. Let's just be safe getting there or we're not going to be of any help at all."

"10-4"

Greg looked in his rearview to see that Eugene was holding his own, towing the boat behind his RV. Agatha was behind him in their truck, and then JJ was bringing up the rear. The caravan of four proceeded like a freight train down the dreadful I-15 until south of Provo where they diverted over to Hwy 89 and proceeded on the quieter two-lane road the rest of the way south.

JJ and Greg were each strategizing on how to find them in the small town. Greg immediately wanted to go to that rental house they'd observed the truck at before, but the police already had confirmed no one was there. And, no sightings of the truck anywhere in town either.

They all had to pull aside in the town of Mt. Pleasant to refuel. After filling and moving his RV to the large overflow parking, JJ came over to help Greg.

"Let's grab some sandwiches inside and keep moving along, what do you say?" JJ asked.

"Definitely. I'm not even hungry, but surely will be before we get there."

"Can you check in with the parents?" Greg grinned as he pointed toward Eugene and Agatha two bays over, "make sure they are doing okay?"

JJ laughed. "They do keep calling us 'the kids', don't they?"

"I was teasing you because Libby told me you have it in your head he could be related."

"Oh that! Well, I think I've dispelled that notion now. I'll fill you in later. Let's go save our women first!" He ran off.

Greg finished filling and just as he tightened the cap, his phone chimed. He quickly grabbed for it in his pocket.

Bring the map and the rest of the loot. Then you get your women back.

Crap, they have Libby's phone!

CHAPTER THIRTY-THREE

Oh nooo!" I whispered, clearly hearing the truck that had pulled up. "Get back over here! We've got to get back on the ground and pretend we're out, or they will drug us again!"

The car doors slammed.

Lexi frantically started hopping back around the toolbox.

The sound of metal against metal clanging at the door … We could hear voices, and I made the 'shh' gesture. We squatted to the floor, reversing the steps we'd just performed, sprawled out on our backs, and prayed we were close to where they'd left us. My heartbeat was banging around in my chest so hard, there was no way we were going to pull this off. Breathe deep, I kept telling myself. I prayed that Lexi was doing the same.

"Libby—I don't think I closed the toolbox drawer…" she whispered.

Shit!

The door to the warehouse opened and bright fluorescent lights flooded the place.

Footsteps moved closer. I could tell now that Todd was dragging his boot as his steps were more labored.

"Good, they're still out," the woman said. I could feel her presence hovering above me and it took everything inside me to be still and regulate my breathing.

"I don't know how. That stuff doesn't usually last *that* long."

"Well, at least they aren't trying to get away … or screaming bloody murder."

"Yeah, Eugene should be here soon with the goods."

"Do you really think the idiot has anything?" she asked. "I mean, I got the coins from him that day in the store. But, has he really found the rest of the family's valuables or have we just been chasing him around the country like dumbasses?"

"I saw the map he had when we were in Escalante. I'm positive now that the big fish clue *has* to reference this lake—*not* the Salt Lake. If it weren't for these guys who keep getting in the way, we'd already have this wrapped up!"

He stopped and I heard him take a few steps away from us.

"Hey! I don't think this was open…" he called out.

"What the hell are you yammerin' on about now?" she asked as she took the few steps over to him.

They both quieted.

I couldn't tell exactly where they were at now, but I kept repeating the mantra 'be still' over and over in my brain. Mantras weren't typically my strong suit—that's Lexi's strength ... so I also continued to pray it was working for her and she wouldn't give us away. The two hoodlums started moving again. Then I got a swift kick in my side. *Ugh!* I used every ounce of my will to not react. From what I could hear, they kicked Alexis as well. She made no sound.

"Nope, not them ... they are *out*!" Todd declared. "Anyway, let's go ... we need to be at the lake pronto! They'll be rollin' into town any time now ... we've gotta take them by surprise and nab that map." He started to hobble away and after one more kick in my side from the woman, it sounded as though she followed him.

"Yep, time to find the real loot, leave no witnesses behind, and get the heck out of Utah!" the graveled voice spoke ominously from a distance.

The light switch clicked, descending us back into darkness as the metal door clanged shut.

The second the truck started up, I rolled to my side, squeezing my arms in around my ribcage and my knees to my chest. "Son of a ..." I moaned. "That HURT! Ugh!"

Alexis agreed with that sentiment too, but was already positioning herself to stand up again. Before I could even sit up, she was standing and moving back around the toolbox, opening drawers like a crazy person.

"Here we go! Screwdrivers, files, so many things ... certainly we can break through these zip ties."

She grabbed several things and scooted back over to sit next to me. Using one of the files she found, she started filing away at the plastic around her feet. I picked up a screwdriver and started working on mine. It wasn't fast, but eventually, we both weakened the plastic ties, breaking them and releasing our feet. We stood up again to walk around the warehouse, looking for anything that would make releasing our hands any easier.

"Over here!" I said, holding up box cutters.

"Perfect!" she smiled.

Alexis held her hands as far apart as possible. I held the cutters firmly and positioned as close to the middle as I could. Holding my breath and praying I wouldn't slip and cut her wrist, I carefully started a sawing motion and the tie released instantly. Alexis did the same thing for me and we were finally free.

"Now, we've got to get out of here. I think they chained that door. But, what about the large rollup doors over there? Is there a switch, or …?" We fumbled our way through the dark to turn on the light switch first. Then we saw the doors more clearly. Only problem was that we didn't see a switch for an automatic opener. We both started banging on the doors and screaming, hoping someone was nearby.

"A crowbar? Maybe we can pry it up enough to lift open?"

We searched all over and didn't find a crowbar, so we started banging and screaming for what felt like hours. In reality, it probably wasn't even a minute. Exhausted, and in pain, we fell to the floor to catch our breath.

"Wait! What was that?" We listened intently.

A car engine. We jumped up and started banging and screaming again.

When we stopped to listen, I asked Alexa, "What if it's *them*?"

"It's not an obnoxious diesel."

Ah, good point.

We heard tires on gravel. The car was slowing. We

banged as hard as we possibly could, considering our injuries and the pain coursing through our bodies. When we stopped again, I jumped wildly. A man's voice sounded, "Come out with your hands up!"

"WE'RE TRAPPED IN HERE!!! PLEASE HELP!!!" I screamed as loud as I possibly could. "HELLLLP!!" We both screamed.

The officer was at the rollup doors now. "Who's in there?" he asked.

"My name is Alexis Johnson and I'm here with Libby Madsen. We were kidnapped, tied up, drugged, and stashed here. Please open these doors and let us out."

"Alexis, Libby … thank goodness we've found you. Hold on, we'll get you out." There were several voices and a ton of activity going on outside the warehouse.

We jumped toward each other and high-fived. Forgetting entirely about our pain, we were so relieved to be rescued. Then, it hit me. *What if these aren't cops on the other side of the door?*

CHAPTER THIRTY-FOUR

Greg had received another text shortly after they pulled out of Mt. Pleasant.

NO cops. Meet at lake no later than 6 p.m. or they're dead.

He buzzed JJ on the two-way radio and told him about the latest message.

"It's after two, we still have ... what, three hours to go?" JJ checked his watch. "That puts us to town around five and we still need to get with the police."

"They said no cops, JJ." Greg was emphatic.

"I know ... but we *have to*," JJ was desperate to get his wife back. "I already called them, Greg."

Of course! By-the-book JJ, as he was known. Greg sighed. "Okay ... it'll be ok. We need to gather our thoughts when we arrive in Panguitch and before heading to the lake. We have no idea who's watching us, we don't know how many are involved here. We cannot risk the lives of the women we love."

"Exactly why we *have* to involve the police."

"Yes, you win. Okay." Greg caught his breath and then, "Do you remember the RV park that's outside of Panguitch … should be the first thing we come to as we approach town?"

"Yep, Whatcha thinking?"

"I will pull in there. We'll hope we can get three spaces; have the cops meet us there. Then, when we go to the lake, we won't show up as the easiest caravan target this side of the Mississippi—we'll take the Jeep instead. Only way we have any hope of pulling a surprise attack on *them*."

"Gotcha. Calling the sheriff now."

The rest of the drive was excruciatingly slow. There were moments where Greg wished they'd just taken the route all the way down I-15 and cut over using Hwy 20 instead. It'd put them out closer to the lake and, with the higher speed limit, maybe they'd already be there. But, he tried to put his mind at ease and concentrate on driving. Eugene and Agatha were still trooping along in the middle of the caravan.

"Greg, can you hear me?" JJ startled him.

"Yep. What's up?"

"I totally forgot to tell you earlier. When we were getting sandwiches, Eugene said something I think I've just put together."

"Okay. What?"

"He said that Panguitch means 'big fish' … wasn't that the final clue?"

"Holy…" Greg couldn't believe what he heard. "You

mean to tell me it's been under our noses and the treasure could have been found earlier this week!"

"Not sure, man. But, sitting here thinking … it makes sense why we're headed back there now."

They pulled up to the RV Resort just outside of Panguitch shortly before five. The hosts already had everything in place for them and escorted them right to their campsites. There were three sheriff's unmarked vehicles also waiting for them.

"Good to meet you, I'm Greg Lawson," he greeted the officers one by one. "This is Shadow, my friend JJ— who you've spoken to by phone, I take it. And, this is Eugene. He's the one they're ultimately after. His family has been searching from some heirlooms and the people who took our wives apparently want those valuables. From everything we've been through so far, we think they are definitely dangerous. We're unsure whether they are armed though."

The officers quickly laid out a plan. They didn't think we should arrive in any car that they potentially had been seen in to date, so they each hopped into separate unmarked police vehicles.

Eugene was in the lead car with two officers. JJ and Greg rode with another officer. Agatha gladly stayed behind at the RV park, shaking her head, as though wondering what all this business was about anyway. Before Greg and JJ's car approached the turnoff to the lake, the officer veered off onto a dirt road.

"Hey! Where are you going?" JJ was quick to react.

"Trust me. Those officers will take good care of your friend. We have some other business to take care of on the way."

Greg's heart sunk as he considered the mess they were

in. *Have we gotten ourselves into a trap? How do we even know for certain these are officers?*

CHAPTER THIRTY-FIVE

I heard what could be a tractor, or a forklift, start up. We instinctively backed away from the garage doors. We each found something heavy to use as a weapon *just in case*. No sooner than we had, two forks poked through, scraping the concrete below the door. They raised the forklift and slowly the door came up. There were several vehicles with their headlights shining right in our faces. Our arms went up to block the blinding light.

We saw several men. Startled, we began to back up further into the warehouse. Then, my eyes must have adjusted because I saw them clearly—Shadow was running, she barked. That's when I saw JJ and Greg coming our way too.

JJ ran and picked up Alexis and she sobbed immediately. Shadow nearly knocked me over. Greg waited for just a moment while I hugged my girl. Then, he took me in his arms and squeezed so tight that I let out a cry. I hugged him back. His lips found mine and we kissed. Then, I pulled back a little, "Ouch, my ribs. I'm so sore!"

"Oh dear, I'm sorry. Let's go get you help."

"No!" both Alexis and I answered sternly. "We have to go get them! They said they're headed to the lake." *How long ago was that anyway?* Then, I looked all around, "Wait, where's Eugene?"

An officer stepped up and answered, "He's with two of our partners. Don't worry, he's safe."

"They will only accept dealing directly with him." I was certain that if a bunch of cops showed up, these two would freak. What would they do to our precious new friend?

Greg touched my forearm, "Hon, did they have guns?"

I shook my head no, "At least I didn't see any. But, they had us drugged, and most of the time, we were wrapped in tarps riding in the back of that ... that, *truck*."

Alexis interrupted, "Please, we want to see these guys apprehended! Let's go!"

After a short briefing between the officers, everyone jumped in a myriad of vehicles and dirt was thrown everywhere as the cars peeled out of the parking lot. On the radio in the car that Greg, Shadow, and I rode in, officers were saying they had spotted the duo in their lifted truck on the farthest southern end of the lake.

"How far away are we?" I asked.

"Fifteen minutes," the officer stated.

The radio buzzed again. From JJ's car, they confirmed the text message was received and Eugene had already been let out on West Shore Road, just before Blue Spring Creek. All other officers were assigned different vantage points.

My eyes found Greg's and there was panic in both of ours. What kind of danger was our friend in?

"Folks, we're assigned to Eagle Lane, very close to your friend. Just so you know, the perpetrators are surrounded in this location and there's no way out for them—by vehicle, anyway."

When we pulled up to our assigned spot, I expected to see tons of police activity. Or something—anything. It was dark and deserted—a quiet tiny lake community, where we parked in the middle of an intersection blocking the road. I didn't see a blue truck.

"Where is everybody?" I quietly asked the officer.

"You won't see any of our guys."

We waited for what felt like an interminable period of time. Then, I saw a single flashlight beam. It was Eugene casually walking alongside the road. I smiled to myself when I saw his perfectly coifed white hair and his stoic ramrod posture. He wore his trademark long-sleeve button down shirt and Levi's along with cowboy boots. He definitely looked like someone straight off a western ranch and not someone who was part of a stakeout.

He stepped off the road and into some shrubbery and we could no longer see him.

"Wait, where did he go?" I was frantic. "Someone needs to get to him."

The officer was now showing signs of losing his patience with me. "It's okay. He has a mic on; our officers can hear anything that he says. And trust me, there are eyes on him and the perpetrators."

I looked to Greg to say something. I didn't believe they were keeping Eugene safe. He just shrugged like, *what can we do?*

The radio crackled. "We have movement. Hold your positions."

I heard the shots before the radio sounded again.

"Shots fired! Repeat, shots fired! All officers move in."

Shadow barked. Our officer leapt from the car and ran off toward the creek. Shadow leapt over the front seat and through the wide-open door, she bolted.

My heart stopped.

CHAPTER THIRTY-SIX

It wasn't two seconds after Shadow ran, my door flew open and I was on the move.

"Libby! No!!!" Greg shouted.

Fortunately, I didn't get far. Every muscle in my body screamed. Cramping around my ribs made me double over in pain.

Shots fired again. I fell to the ground.

Greg got out and slunk around the car staying low to the ground. He got to me, and helped me up. "Stay low," he instructed, and helped me around to the other side of the car. We peeped up to see through the windows. There still was nothing to see.

We could hear the radio though and an officer confirmed they had the two suspects. Another officer, I presumed was our driver, said they couldn't find Eugene. I stood up, gripping my side, "C'mon … let's go find him."

Greg and I walked across the road and along the creek where we'd seen Eugene disappear. As we stepped through the thick shrubbery, the rough-looking woman was being led out in handcuffs. Her steely glare met mine. I couldn't help myself—I kicked her right in the shin. Shadow barked at her and the officer scowled at me.

"Bitch!" she growled at me. The officer pushed her to continue moving.

"Where's Eugene?" I yelled after her. "What have you done with our friend?"

The officer indicated they were looking for him and Todd had been detained. Then he pushed on by us and hauled her to the squad car that pulled up. We continued following along the path in the dim light through the shrubbery.

It was tall and thick in places. "Shadow!" I yelled out. Greg screamed for Eugene. We kept our eyes open for more officers too. Since they had their suspects, we just hoped no more shots would be fired. We followed the creek along, continuously calling out for my baby and our friend. Coming up on a lava field, we carefully navigated, walking among loose rock.

We both heard the bark and turned around. She barked again.

"I think she's just over that ridge right there!" I started moving quicker, climbing up the lava rock hill and then carefully taking it slow coming down the other side. There was scratchy scrub brush everywhere. "Where are you, girl?" I called out. "Shadow!"

She was barking continuously now. Then I saw a wiggle in the bushes just ahead of us, and I knew she was close.

As we thrashed to get through, another officer met up with us, also following the sound of the bark. There was Shadow, huddled up next to Eugene, who had apparently fallen. She jumped up, wriggling about with an excited whine. I leaned down to praise her and then she went right back to Eugene's side. The officer stepped away to radio in their location.

I rushed up to him. "Are you okay?" I looked around and the elderly man was leaning on another mound of lava flow. On the ground, he suddenly looked small to me; I got worried. I knelt down at his side. "Are you injured, Eugene?"

"Oh no, nothing that bad. Just rolled my ankle a little, I think. It was the gunfire that made me stay down here. Did they get 'em?" His eyes shone bright at the prospect of shooting down the bad guys, and I just had to laugh.

"Well, I'm glad Shadow found you!" Greg moved in and tried to help him up.

He started to whisper. "Oh no, I'm not getting up. It's right here!" He pointed to the lava flow.

"What's right there?"

He waved us in closer, continuing to whisper. "We have to mark this place. The treasure—it's here." He pointed to a cave-like portion in the ancient molten flow. I peered in and it did look like the cave was quite large.

"Hurry, that officer will be right back. Shhhhh." He pulled a bunch of wiring from behind his back. "Don't worry, I took it off once they grabbed Todd, and, and, that beastly … *woman*."

"It's okay, why are you worried about the police?"

"Well, since this is a scene of a crime now, I don't want them confiscating all of Evelyn's stuff!" He sounded angry all of a sudden.

I hadn't thought about that, so maybe he had a good point. Greg nodded in agreement too.

"Okay, let's get you up and make sure you can walk out of here. We'll mark our way out so you know where to come back to."

"Don't worry about that now. I've got the map!" He glistened again.

Greg helped lift Eugene to standing. He put his weight on his legs and was good to go—no pain at all. I wished I could say the same, but I was motivated to get out of here and find out about the arrests that were being made.

Greg was curious, "Eugene, were Todd and Charley here at the cave when you found them?"

"Yup. She's a mean young'un … whew, don't want to run across her ever again. And, to think she's claiming to be my daughter! No way, no how!" He shook his head vehemently denying he was related to such evil. "She's greedy, conniving, and just looking for an easy buck. No scruples at all."

Greg chuckled a bit at the description of the woman they'd followed here. I understood exactly what Eugene was talking about, as I felt the side of my ribcage again. Ouch!

Partway back, walking through the sand in the creek bed, the officer who drove us to Eagle Lane was walking toward us.

"I thought I told you to stay in the car!" he admonished us.

"Sorry! You left the door opened and my dog jumped out and ran to find him." I pointed to Eugene. "Where did you go? I thought you'd get to him before us?"

"Ah, apparently the suspects had taken off running." He indicated they headed east from here. "Our officers had found their truck just down the way. And, of course, that's the direction they were headed when we took them down."

"Who fired shots?"

"Our officers. Unfortunately, the male suspect reached into his jacket and brandished a weapon. After repeated requests to drop it and put his hands up, the officers fired. He had pointed his weapon right at them, they had no choice."

My brain went back to the warehouse. *So, they had weapons all along?* I shuddered to think what could have happened to us.

"Don't worry," the officer said, seeing the look of horror on my face. "We got him in the leg ... just enough to take him down. He'll be alright. The little lady, as tough a talker as she was, gave up right away. That was easy."

"We'd have found this guy a little sooner had he not taken off his surveillance equipment!" the officer admonished Eugene.

The older man just smiled feigning lack of hearing. I knew better, and chuckled to myself.

It was a very long night at the sheriff's substation. We all gave our statements and waited for the others to finish. Finally, sometime after midnight, we were taken back to the RV Resort just outside Panguitch town limits. Agatha came running out and gave Eugene an enormous hug.

"I was so worried, honey," she cried openly.

After their embrace, she gave each of us each hugs

too. "I thank you for saving my man's life! I'm so happy we met you guys when we did. You've *saved* him!" She kept repeating that sentiment many times until, finally, the two of them disappeared into their RV for the rest of the night.

Alexis looked beat and JJ hovered over her—I wondered if he'd ever leave her side again. Greg and I were equally exhausted, but first, we walked with our friends several spots down the lane to their RV before we ventured over to ours.

JJ sighed, "So, tomorrow morning—heading back to Arizona?"

I smiled, looked to Greg, then back at JJ with a devious grin. "Not quite. One more thing left to do first."

He looked confused. I held up my hands and started to back up. "It's a secret. We will learn more in the morning. Get a good night's sleep." I looked to Alexis who appeared she was just done with us. "Take some Advil, some chamomile tea, and rest, sweetie. Tomorrow's adventure will be fun."

They both looked at us helplessly as we walked away. I felt bad not saying more now, but I knew I'd be forgiven by morning.

CHAPTER THIRTY-SEVEN

Eugene and Agatha took the lead in their truck and the rest of us followed in the Jeep.

"I don't understand. Why are we going back to the scene of the crime?" Alexis asked skeptically.

"Just wait— you'll see," I teased. Greg took my hand and squeezed as he made the turn onto West Shore Road. We pulled up behind Eugene on the shoulder of the road, just where Blue Spring crossed below us.

The second that JJ opened the door, Shadow jumped out and ran to Eugene.

"Well, hello there my friend," he said sweetly and petted her. "Are you ready to find the treasure today?"

Alexis and JJ overheard him and looked to Greg and me with wide eyes.

Agatha rolled her eyes. "Yep, today's the day!" I took

it as sarcasm, but who knows, maybe she was as excited as Eugene. In her own way.

"C'mon gang, follow me."

As we walked through the creek bed and navigated the lava flow again, I was extremely impressed with Eugene's sense of direction. He walked right to where we found him yesterday.

He turned to Greg, "Got that flashlight?" He handed it over and Eugene shined it into the cave. Ducking down, he slowly crept, hunched over, into the dark lava cavern. Our overly excited canine dashed by him and disappeared into the shadows. I followed in after Eugene and one by one, each of us entered the tunnel. It was far larger than I originally had thought, and we must have walked twenty yards or so before we heard Shadow barking.

Eugene got to her first; she was digging furiously and kicking up sand. JJ skirted around us.

"Here's the shovel you had me carry." He handed it to Eugene.

The old man started digging. When he stopped, Greg and JJ each took turns. Eventually, we all stood aside and stared into the approximately three-foot deep hole in the ground. The smile on Eugene's face was priceless. He hopped down into the hole, followed by Greg. JJ was still down there. Together the three of them lifted out a huge chest. To me, it looked more like a trunk that one would have used to haul their belongings across on a long ocean sailing back in the 1880s. Once they had it freed from the sand, the two men stepped back and motioned for Eugene to take the honor of opening it.

He used all his might and barely budged the lid. Greg stepped over and using the shovel, he was able to get the edge just in the seam and pried it apart. Then, he moved out of the way and let Eugene do the reveal.

Agatha's eyes widened in amazement as she shined her flashlight into the chest. I leaned closer and my hands went straight to my mouth.

Eugene's eyes were humongous and I'd never seen a wider smile consume his face. He leaned down and pulled out a gold bar in one hand and a silver bar in the other. He lifted them high above his head.

"We did it!!!" he yelled out. "We found Evelyn's family's fortune!"

It took all of us to heft the chest out of the three-foot hole—it was extraordinarily heavy. Once we did that, Greg and JJ hiked back to the Jeep and retrieved our four backpacks and some tow straps. With the straps, we were able to drag the chest through the sand, closer to the cave entrance. Then, the four of us spent the rest of the day hauling out the loot in our backpacks. The men handled the heaviest items. Alexis and I hauled lighter loads, as we were still extremely sore, but we managed the short hike numerous times fairly well. We left Eugene and Agatha at the cars to stand guard until we got everything out.

Eugene came up to us after our last load. He hugged me and Alexis, and shook the guys' hands. "I could never have done all this without you. I'm so grateful to you all, my newfound friends!"

"I'm shocked you found actual treasure!" I said, laughing. He didn't laugh along.

"You didn't believe me?" he said, wounded.

"Oh! Uh, no ... of course, I believed you. I'm just surprised..." I waved my hands back toward the creek bed. "I mean, *how* did you figure it was *here*?"

He smiled. "Well, of course, that's a long story … let's go back to the camp and I'll tell you all!"

CHAPTER THIRTY-EIGHT

In the end, we helped Eugene count his findings. In that chest were: fifty gold bars; a hundred silver bars; stacks of cash (that hadn't been counted yet); numerous leather pouches of old Civil War era coins; and most importantly, Eugene found the watch that Evelyn had always talked about. I personally didn't see anything special about the watch—it looked extremely old and worn. But, if it was important to him, I was thrilled he finally found it after all these years.

Eugene saw me eyeing the watch. He sidled over to me, flipped it over and showed me the back. Inscribed on the back: *Robert E. Lee 1865*. My jaw dropped and I looked to Eugene. "Yep, *the* war General himself. This is what was so important to Evelyn." He turned the watch over and over in his hands, examining it. "Now, I can't remember the exact familial relationship, but Evelyn's maiden name was Lee. She was a descendant of—somehow. I'd have to read up to learn more, but I'm not so interested in that. I'm just happy I could fulfill my promise to her."

My eyes had welled up with tears as I listened to him. Greg was tending to the fire; Agatha, Alexis, and JJ all sat nearby.

JJ broke the silence that had fallen over us. "Okay, how did Todd and Charley play into *any* of this?"

Eugene cleared his throat. "Well, apparently ... I learned when they started fighting in front of me and the police ... Charley was an old girlfriend of Todd's. As you learned earlier on this trip, Todd is Evelyn's nephew. His father spoke a lot about these fortunes. Over the course of the years, and after I'd come to learn he was hiding the fortune as a ... oh, I don't know, hobby? I still can't understand what he was doing ... but, as Todd grew up, he was also hell-bent on finding this stuff. It sounds like he must have told the girlfriend at some point." He stopped to take a sip of his beer. "Well, even many years after they'd broken up, her greed and questionable moral compass got the better of her. Todd said something about trying to protect *me* from *her* ... so even though he was still looking for the treasure, he'd been threatened by her and learned that she was out to get *me*. Probably as a way to get to the loot, I'm sure."

"So, why didn't he just come out and tell you about her? Why not be up front?" I asked.

He shook his head in disgust. "Libby, Todd is not a good man. You're right, he could have been straight with us from the beginning. No, I believe he followed me ... connected with me only to swindle. Then, once he realized she'd found both of us, his story conveniently changed—and in front of the officers, mind you."

Greg sighed. "Why did they steal our ladies?"

JJ choked on his beer. "I spoke with the commander a little bit ago. Todd confessed that ploy was only to get to you, Eugene. They knew we'd all come running."

Alexis then added, "Okay … then I don't understand what all that craziness was in Park City? Who came after the two of you on the ski hills?" she looked to Greg and JJ.

JJ knew about that too. "Apparently, the two were arguing during their arrest and Charley mentioned they should have 'had the same kids' take the ladies and not have gotten involved in that. When questioned further, they actually admitted they had some locals in Park City try to scare us off. They didn't want us all to continue on to Salt Lake. It would be easier to swindle Eugene without the rest of us."

I furrowed my brows. "I don't understand the warnings that I was getting then. The warnings were seemingly threats *toward* Eugene … that would only make us want to help him even more, right?"

Eugene laughed. "You say that like they're smart people, Libby."

We all busted out laughing. He had a point.

"Okay, but the biggest question is … *how* did you know about that cave? *When* did you figure it out? Or, you would have just found it during the first trip through Panguitch, right?"

Eugene sat back in his chair and crossed his hands over his belly. "You are right, Libby. I missed a lot early on in the trip. I had found the final two clues at Lake Powell: Salton Sea and Big Fish. I had no idea what they meant or even how to proceed. However, as I mentioned before, the 'pass the salt' *warning* made me think of Salt Lake City. How? I can't say … it just got in my head. Then, I remembered something Evelyn told me years ago about Antelope Island … and, I knew to go there. We found the coins so I knew we were on the right path. Her brother hid bits and pieces of the whole treasure to lure us along."

He stopped, looked around at everyone, and then continued, "After you ladies disappeared, and we got the text to go to Panguitch … well, we were at the gas station, I picked up a brochure on Panguitch Lake in one of those 'Things To Do" in the region displays. Right there, it said 'Panguitch—whose name means *big fish*' and then went on to talk about the great fishing at the lake. It also mentioned lava flows and caves. Evelyn's family used to vacation in this region and I remembered stories she told of swimming into lava caves. Now, I didn't ever remember her saying 'Panguitch' specifically … no, that was indeed a long shot for me."

"Wouldn't Todd have immediately known that?" Alexis added.

"Not necessarily. He and his Dad were estranged for many years. He had a lot of catch up to do on family history. I'm sure I knew more than he did."

I still didn't understand. "But, how did you know specifically which lava cave?"

"Oh, I had numerous maps I'd found from clues over the years. But, you have to understand that until I found the last two clues—at Powell—the maps seemed worthless to me. In the end, Todd asking to meet where he did, that was the moment I knew to grab the map before we headed off with the officer." He pulled the map from his back pocket. "I knew it was at a lake … see here. But, until I tied this Panguitch Lake to this map, and then specifically the part of the lake that Todd asked for us to meet him—well, let's just say Evelyn's brother did a fantastic job hiding it all these years!"

It was all so much. After an extremely long day, I'd lost all energy and needed to lie down. Everyone was in agreement and we called it a night.

The next day, we packed up early and all three camps caravanned to Lake Powell. It was a great stopping point before we split up—Eugene and Agatha headed to Colorado Springs and us back to Mesa. By this time, the older couple felt like family to us. Agatha had settled down now that Eugene was content and the treasure hunt was complete. We gathered one last time in Page at the restaurant where the whole group met initially. A different cover band was playing country tunes and we couldn't keep Eugene and Agatha from the dance floor. Shadow kept her eyes on them the entire time—they were adorable.

When we got back to the campsite, Eugene pulled me aside and asked, "Before we all take off in the morning, there's one last thing I'd like to do. Will you guys come with me?"

"Sure, Eugene. We'd like to get an early start though—can we do whatever it is you need us for really early?"

"Yep, yep … prefer it that way. Thanks, Libby!"

In the morning, we followed Eugene to a beautiful bluff overlooking the Glen Canyon Dam. Agatha had elected to stay back at the park so it was Alexis, JJ, Greg, Eugene, Shadow and me crowded into the Jeep. We parked at the end of a road and then walked to the top of the cliff. He had Greg carry a container in his backpack. When we got to the top, Eugene started looking all around.

"Ah, there it is." He walked over several yards, we followed. Then, I saw it … a marker in the ground.

"What is this, Eugene?" I asked.

"This is where Evelyn wanted her final resting place." He motioned for Greg's backpack. Then, looked to JJ. "Shovel?"

"Yep, got it." He held it up.

Eugene dug a really small hole quickly. Then, he asked everyone to gather around. He licked his finger and held it up, testing for wind.

"Okay, stand here…" we all stood toward the east where the sun was about to rise. He bowed his head and we followed suit. "Dearest Evelyn, by now you know that I found what your father meant for you to have. I told you I wouldn't leave this earth before accomplishing that!" He chuckled. Then his voice cracked, "I love you dearly, sweetheart. You were my only soulmate, my true love. I hope you've always known that; it won't be long now, darling."

Tears were flowing down my face. I looked over to the others and no one had dry eyes. Eugene knelt down, took the watch off his wrist and put it in the hole he'd just dug. After filling the hole in with dirt, he opened the box and pulled out an urn. He tested the wind once again and nodded our way. We all held hands as he emptied the urn; we watched the dust float off into the distance and over the lake. I couldn't contain my emotions—I wept openly as I felt the significance of Eugene's devotion to Evelyn and the profound loving gesture he had just carried out. That was only amplified by the love I saw between Agatha and Eugene when we arrived back at the campground. I probably never would understand their relationship, or how Agatha handled all the years of Eugene's obsession, but what was clear—there was immense love between them as well.

CHAPTER THIRTY-NINE

I got the call a week after we had arrived back home. Shadow nudged me awake to answer the call.

It had been a quiet drive home; all of our energy had been spent on what turned out to be a vacation we'd never forget. No, it wasn't *exactly* the vacation we'd planned, but I wouldn't have changed it for the world. We met lifelong friends and were included to experience things most people never would in their entire lifetime.

Eugene, at ninety-five years old, was a truly remarkable man. His stamina, his morals and ethics, his devotion, his optimism, and his ability to find humor in not-so-great situations. That's what he'd be remembered for. He was an adventurer—unafraid to live life; he sought out more in life than people half his age would ever dream of. I'll never forget him.

Once I got dressed, I called Alexis and JJ. They were awake and I was to come straight over.

Alexis took me in her embrace and didn't let go for several minutes. Our shoulders heaved as we cried onto each other.

JJ started to dial Greg's number. When he answered, we all sat on the sofa with Greg on speaker phone.

"Hon," my voice cracked, "Eugene passed away in his sleep overnight."

"Oh no!" Greg exclaimed.

Alexis and I couldn't stop crying. Finally, I choked out the words, "I think that's what he meant when he told Evelyn, 'It won't be long darling'..." I lost it again.

We all sat around telling stories from our recent trip with Eugene. We laughed; we sobbed. Then, we called Agatha and pulled her in on a three-way call. There weren't going to be formal services, but we asked if there was anything we could do for her. We offered for her to come to Arizona and get away for a while, if she needed to. She thanked us all, and said she probably would visit at some point down the line, but we weren't to worry—she had a lot of her family around and she'd be just fine. I really hoped that would be the case.

Several weeks later, I received a box in the mail. Upon opening, there was a note just inside the flap. It said, "*The kids will know exactly where to put me.*" And then there was another note. "*Libby, he left this note in his nightstand drawer. You and your friends are the only 'kids' he'd be referring to—please take good care with him. Love, Agatha.*"

I opened the next flap and saw that it was an urn. Shadow came over and stuck her head into the box. With tears running down my cheek, Shadow licked my face and then curled up next to me on the couch. I smiled and closed the lid. I knew *exactly* where we'd take him.

Thank you for taking the time to read *Shadowed Treasures*. If you enjoyed it please tell your friends, and I would be so grateful if you would consider posting a review. Word of mouth is an author's best friend, and very much appreciated.

Thank you,

Jennifer Morgan

* * *

Get another free book from Jennifer—click here to find out how!

Books in the Libby Madsen Cozy Mysteries series:

Shadows in the Forest
Spa Shadows
Shadowed Treasures
Shadow Retreats (fall/winter, 2022)
The Christmas Fairy – a holiday novella

Scan the QR code to see them all!

What's next for Libby and Shadow?

Libby becomes concerned when her friend, Bella Crenshaw, shares details about a group that she's recently joined and has embraced. Love & Mercy proclaims to be a new-age, self-help, religious organization. It's the latest enlightenment craze amongst the Hollywood elite; they have many branches around the country, including in Southern Arizona.

Kali Patel is the most sought-after guru and leader of Love & Mercy. Devoted members have followed her, and her second in command, Uma Devi, for years—drawn in droves to their essence as well as their teachings.

Bella convinces Libby to join her for the highly anticipated annual retreat weekend—all are welcome, and with the cute cabin setup, Shadow can come along. What Libby discovers once she's there is frightening. Is this a legit religious organization? To Libby, it certainly appears to be a dangerous cult.

Members begin to disappear, along with millions of dollars. It's only when Bella's newest friend at the center, the beautiful California girl, Jill Walsh, begins displaying disturbing behavior, that Bella also questions the organization. What has she gotten herself into now? And can Libby and Shadow somehow figure out what's behind the disappearances before something terrible happens to her friend?

Watch for *Shadow Retreats,* **coming soon!**

Jennifer J. Morgan grew up in the desert Southwest where she always dreamed of becoming an author. Raised in New Mexico, and currently living in Arizona, she is a desert dweller through and through. Similar to her protagonist, Libby Madsen, she loves traveling and adventure.

When she's not writing, Jennifer enjoys camping, hiking, and traveling with her husband and two dogs. She is also an arts and crafts nut, always taking on a new project that sparks her creativity.

Fun fact: Most of her characters in the Libby Madsen Cozy Mystery are named after beloved pets that have blessed her life over fifty+ years. She is a HUGE animal lover (dogs, cats, birds...). Given the chance, she'd rescue them all (including a few goats, chickens, ducks, you name it...). Or, as she likes to say, her animals have always rescued her.

Let's connect!

Website: jenniferjmorgan.com
Email: jennifer@jenniferjmorgan.com
Facebook: https://www.facebook.com/profile.
php?id=100076154359528
Twitter: JenniferJMorga3
BookBub: bookbub.com/profile/433830544
Goodreads: 148099219-jennifer-morgan